WHEN THE ANGELS HAVE RISEN

by
ANDREW FEDER

authorHOUSE™

1663 LIBERTY DRIVE, SUITE 200
BLOOMINGTON, INDIANA 47403
(800) 839-8640
WWW.AUTHORHOUSE.COM

First published by AuthorHouse 05/23/05

ISBN: 1-4208-3041-4 (sc)

Library of Congress Control Number: 2005904304

Printed in the United States of America
Bloomington, Indiana

This book is printed on acid-free paper.

In memory of my father, Perry Feder, my brother, Eric Feder and my teacher and guide,
Janaeu St. Clair...

I also dedicate this book to my loving children, Rachel, Michelle and Perry along with the knowledge and wisdom from Janeau and Elliot. I thank G-d and the universe for this loving opportunity and the path toward knowledge and wisdom with love and LIGHT.

TABLE OF CONTENTS

CHAPTER 1

IN THE BEGINNING....

Genesis 1:00

When G-d began to create the heaven and the earth—the earth being unformed and void, with darkness over the surface of the deep and a wind from G-d sweeping over the water—G-d said, "Let there be light"; and there was light. G-d saw that light was good, and G-d separated the light from the darkness.

Looking back....

I was on Highway Fifteen cruising from Los Angeles to the city of sin known as Las Vegas.

It was such a beautiful evening that I could feel the cool desert summer night breeze stroking my face. And while taking a deep breath, I could smell the fresh, clean desert air, which was something refreshing—that is, for a native Angeleno. As much as they have tried to clean the air in Los Angeles, the brown-orange cloud of smog still remained a constant with its choking skies.

That evening, during my journey, there were so many stars brilliantly lighting the desert nightscape that one could even drive without using one's headlights. And there was also nothing like driving on a summer night with the illuminating full moon cascading light upon the desert frontier. I felt like I was in one of those movies. It was all so surreal, but then life has some surrealism to it, doesn't it?

What was that? How strange. From the eastern horizon, an unusual violet glow had suddenly appeared and then disappeared. Well, whatever, I guessed that it was expected to see unusual things in the desert, especially if you're driving by yourself, all alone. Yeah, I was alone on this journey. One might say that we're always alone when we make any sudden change or changes in one's journey in life. And like someone said, "You're born alone and you die alone." Whatever that means...

But I had wondered... As a forty-two-year-old previously divorced man, will this journey be a new start or just a breath of fresh air? Or was this the preamble of a midlife crisis? No matter. I was hoping it would be a new start. At least that's what I thought. So I was heading to Las Vegas with its mirage of hope and dreams.

Oh, man! My bladder felt like it was about to burst. Thank God for the small town of Baker, known for its big buns, a crazy Greek, and you guessed it. This town has the largest thermometer in the world, and should I say more. Ouch, my asshole hurts just from thinking about it. So I pulled off to relieve myself. In other words, I took a piss.

Well, this was my last "piss" stop before crossing into the Silver State known as Nevada. While pulling into the convenience store, "AM-PM," I glanced at my watch. It was now nine o'clock...

Now what was the reason for my exile? Well, I didn't leave the City of Angels, because I hated Los Angeles. No. For the truth of the matter, I truly loved the city... In fact, I was going to miss my two children. My son and younger daughter both lived with their mother in Westlake Village, while my older daughter, Roxanne, whom I had raised, was now living with her boyfriend in Vegas.

I was also going to miss my sweetheart, Joanne. We'd just broken up for convenience sake. I was at an all-time low, and this was definitely affecting our relationship. And so it was best for the both of us that we separated. And this separation gave me the opportunity to move on and start anew.

But the main reason for my sudden exodus was, like many in this country, I became a victim of the injustice in our present legal system. I had been convicted for not complying with a court order. In other words, I was found guilty of contempt of court. How ironic. I was found guilty of contempt in a contemptuous court. Though in a prior hearing, a judge had told me to pay the "minimum" of five hundred dollars per month toward child support, and I did make those payments, an overzealous prosecutor trying to win one, whatever the consequences, managed to convince the criminal judge in the monkey court, if you can call it that... Well, the judge basically went along with whatever the prosecutor had suggested without any consideration to the truth or a fair trial, and thus the testimony from the prior hearing that I just mentioned was stricken to be heard by the jury. And so, I was found in contempt of not complying with a prior order. I could go on and on in more specifics of my case, but what would be the point? The family courts are full of clowns and monkeys, if you get my drift... So, I thought that I had two choices, either I leave the State of California, or I continue to head in a downward spiral while being sucked down the tube of double standards in what was considered politically correct. So, like a lot of people in midlife crisis, I needed a sudden a change, or rather perhaps a detour... But my detour was not emancipation, but rather an exile to a new life. So it was escape to Las Vegas for me.

And right then, my fucking bladder was about to explode, so I really, I mean that I *really* had to TAKE A FUCKING PISS!!!

After pissing like a racehorse, I hopped back into my old, beat-up 1978 black BMW and continued on my journey to the oasis of Las Vegas. Again I glanced at my watch, and it was now nine fifteen.

10:00 PM...

I continued cruising, but suddenly within the night sky overhead, an enormous brilliant bluish-white light had quickly engulfed my car and then vanished. I glanced at my energy drink, the "Red Bull." Maybe the "Red Bull" that I had just drunk was starting to kick in. Hey, anything with several grams of niacin, vitamin B-12, vitamin B-6, and caffeine would certainly kick anyone's ass. Well, it didn't make me fly like I had wings, but it indeed woke my ass up, and I was buzzing like no tomorrow. And no, I wasn't on a "Fear and Loathing" tour either, and no, I wasn't having any kind of LSD flashback. So though I was just tweaking some bit from my "Red Bull," I was still maintaining. That is, I was in control. At least, that's what I thought...

Again, a sudden, flash of bluish-white light had engulfed my car. Again I looked at my can of "Red Bull." Nope, it certainly wasn't the drink as I tossed the empty can to the floor behind my seat.

So to pass the time, I flicked on the radio, but the announcer had cut off the song that was playing and then gave a news update. That's all needed now a fucking news update. "Update this!" I replied to radio like it could see me when I flipped off my middle finger.

Well, apparently, violence in the Mid-East had subsided while the Israelis and Palestinians had surprisingly continued their talks of peace.

3

Also, President Halliburton had just declared an expansion of his newfound Department of Homeland Security. All the while, sporadic protests against corporate globalization had begun to emerge across the world. And what seemed at the time most unusual, the world was going through its third global "El Nino" in a row. Unusual weather patterns had continued to persist. Namely, there was an unusual amount of rain in deserts and arid areas, while in the temperate regions, there was less rainfall and more warm weather.

Ah, fuck. Enough of that crap. I had my own fucking life to straighten out. So I turned off the radio as if that would have stopped what was unfolding around the world. During my approach to Las Vegas, one could have seen the reddish streaming sunlight coming through from the eastern horizon. I gazed at my watch. It was displaying 6:05. Huh? That was fucking weird... I had been driving for eight hours, but by car from Baker to Las Vegas was only an hour and half drive, and yet I had lost six and half hours. How bizarre. Oh, well, I must've blacked out.

I glanced at the "Red Bull," and said to myself, "I'm not going to drink that shit no more." But then again, strange things do happen when one travels on the "I-15" to Las Vegas at night **alone.**

Oh, by the way, I'm Jerry... Jerry Fletcher...

CHAPTER 2

AT PRESENT

Well, first thing I did when I got to Las Vegas was to do the standard thing—look for an apartment and, of course, a fucking job. In Vegas, both are pretty easy to accomplish, and before the "Great Recession," you could basically fall down and find a job. Well, the job I had found was telemarketing... Yeap, I was one of those pesky assholes that would bug the shit out of you while you were simply trying to have nice quiet dinner with your family while I in the meanwhile was busy trying to sell you some fucking long distance.

Well, anyway, during my illustrious career in the long distance business, I went back to school to learn graphic art. And after six months, I graduated with a certificate and all, and thus got a new job in my new career as a graphic artist. I became your typical working nine-to-fiver "schnook" having the same mirage of every blue blue-collared working schnook thinking that all that mattered in life was financial security. So I continued my new nine-to-five life. It was a first, since I had really never worked for anyone but for myself...

Right after college, for six years, I had lived in Israel raising grapes and fruit on my farm. Because of my father's poor health, I came back to the United States, where I was very much involved with the family business. My family had owned a film studio and a distribution company, but the legal mafia, the Internal Revenue Service, had sunk in their fangs only to kill the tree which provided the very fruit which supported 300 employees, but again that's a whole story unto itself and a very political one, at that.

After the IRS H-bombed my family's business, during the next nine years, I got into the insurance repair business (repairing homes and commercial buildings after a fire or other catastrophic disaster) until... Well, until my contractor's license was temporarily suspended by the Los Angeles County District Attorney's Office which ultimately destroyed my business. But enough of that... I was starting a whole new life, leaving all that had passed into the past.

Eight months later...

I had begun to work designing signage in the graphics department of a very large corporation that provided services for convention shows in Las Vegas.

It was in a large warehouse atmosphere; as you entered the graphics department area, to your immediate left was the administrative area, where the clerical operations were handled. In the center of the facility, there were rows of tables where the graphic prints were applied to their appropriate substrate. And at the rear of the facility, there were laminators where the prints are laminated prior to being applied to their substrate. While at the right side of the facility, there were computer stations of graphic artists, including myself where layouts were prepared. Adjacent to these stations were eight "Encad Novajet" printers. Now on the opposite side of the facility, there were small offices where the project managers and the graphics department manager were located.

Besides laying out designs, I also helped Jed Yoda, who was the printer technician and color manager, in the actual printing of the layouts.

Now, how do I describe Jed? Well, simply speaking, Jed was a Polynesian version of a "troll doll." It was funny because he never would consider himself of Asian descent; rather, he would declare like it was the most important thing for all to know that he was an Islander or Pacific Islander. That's because his mother was from the Philippines and his father was from Guam, but I guess that during these times, people were more concerned with their ethnicity than the real issue that mattered— that being our interrelationship among humanity as a whole.

Though at times Jed could be emotionally very immature, mentally he was quite the intelligent. He recently transferred himself from being my immediate supervisor to an equipment technician. This move opened the door for Marvin to replace him as my immediate supervisor.

Oh, yeah, Marvin. What a character. He was a small, scrawny thing of a man with an ever-growing receding hairline, who was suffering from Napoleonism, the "power trip" that any small man might be privy to and suffer from. His nickname around the shop was "Little Hitler." Power can certainly change people, because Marvin was not at all the Machiavellian type before his promotion. He was a kind and caring man, but power can certainly change that in some individuals.

While sitting and moving my mouse, clicking away on the computer keyboard and viewing my monitor, I was designing an advertisement for signage for an upcoming convention when Jed suddenly yelled out, "Hey, Jerry, could you get me a roll of photo-base!"

While clicking on my keyboard saving the design, I replied, "No problem..."

Within moments, I returned with a forty-two-inch roll of photo-base paper which was to be printed on Encad Novajet printers, which resembled oversized computer inkjet printers. These printers would print the digital layouts.

"Fuckin' 'A' Jed! It stinks like shit! I can't breathe! You fucking putz!" While trying to breathe and squeezing my nostrils shut, I lashed out.

Jed just immaturely chuckled.

Heaven forbid if I breathed in that nasty shit. Jed's farts were so nasty, they could melt the paint off a moving car.

Suddenly, Hank, a forty-year-old man in the shape of a penguin began shouting out loud in his high-pitched voice that resembled flying geese, "That was nothing. Aaaagh!" Hank then grunted out his counter of "mustard gas."

That's fucking great. What a great working environment. I was working alongside two immature grown men who were cutting farts like they were still in boys' camp. "Just keep the matches away from those two..."

From the supervisor's area, Danny scolded back, "Keep it down, you guys!"

"Here's your fucking paper! Why don't both of you just stay over there and keep your farts to yourselves," I snapped back while heading toward the supervisor's area, which was adjacent to the front administrative area.

So from day to day, I pretty much continued doing the same thing over and over again, which was as monotonous as describing where I had worked. In other words, boring... But deep inside, I always felt that this was just perhaps a stepping stone. But what and to where? Maybe this stepping stone was full of gum and I wasn't going anywhere. But at least, I could appreciate that I was not homeless and destitute. We sometimes take things for granted, never appreciating the little things we do have.

But at this time, it was quite hard to understand, let alone empathize, with the life of being a simple part in a simple machine. Like Charlie Chaplin's *Modern Times,* the life of a nine-to-fiver was depressing not only due to the prevalent monotony, but also to the neutering of any real creative endeavors one might wish to pursue. The life of the nine-to-fiver justified the castration of one's real dreams. So as I worked my day in "modern times," I empathized with the underlying depression that lies beneath the psyche of the average worker. I would look into their eyes, and I would see the very demeanor which created where I stood now. My dreams, like theirs, were stifled into oblivion. So I fought within myself to surface my endeavors and my dreams, but where were they now? Because I thought that I knew... I didn't know... Don't we all have dreams? But what would be of my dreams? I really didn't know at that time. So for now, I was searching... Searching for my dream... And for some, this quest would take a lifetime.

Overhead, on a radio, I could hear the news. There was an announcement of a possible flood warning. I looked toward the exterior platform, and there wasn't a cloud in the sky. So much for weathermen... But suddenly out of nowhere, without a cloud in the sky, it had begun to pour.

From the counter, Danny, the lead supervisor shouted, "Hey, Jerry, I got a big job for ya!" I approached the counter and then looked at the plans. "Here, this job is a structure. And here are the specifications of the structure and here is what the client wants." Danny, in his laid back tone, explained while pointing to the plans. Danny thought he was still in the eighties, with his long black hair cut into a mullet like "Joe Dirt."

Oh by the way, Danny loved the St. Louis Rams, the pro football team, so it wasn't a good idea to say anything negative about his team, or you'd end up doing "Mitchell" jobs for a while. In our department, Mitchell jobs were always a cluster fuck, and no one in their right mind wanted to have anything to do with them, so I kept my mouth shut.

Mitchell, a project manager, was a small nerdy man who thought he was the hippest thing on earth. Hell, the guy would come in sometimes all orange from using indoor tanning lotion, wearing khaki shorts in the middle of winter. Mitchell never paid any attention to what he was doing, so his jobs were always a catastrophe.

Danny continued, "So these headers are all inserts, but the panels are overlays. So design the layouts like these thumbnails but with these sizes. Okay?"

"No problem..." I replied.

Suddenly, Keyshawn, a light-skinned African-American and Vietnamese man resembling Tiger Woods, entered the facility.

Danny looked up at the clock. It was ten o'clock.

In a cool manner, Danny reprimanded, "Keyshawn, you're two hours late. After I finish going over this project with Jerry, you and I are going to have a little talk."

"So yo! Like Jerry boy... What's up?" Keyshawn replied, smiling.

"All right... So Keyshawn, how'd you do on the parley?" I asked.

"Man, I lost my ass, thanks to your Lakers."

"Bro, I told you don't... Don't ever bet against my team. You know if you bet against my Lakers, then you might as well be dropping your coin in my pocket, because either way, you're giving up your coin. And for me, I could certainly use some of that spare coin, if you know what I mean... Perhaps, Keyshawn, you would like to donate your future losses to the Jerry Foundation?" I smiled back, and then with the plans and thumbnails in hand, I headed back to my computer station.

Just as I sat down, Sherry cursed out, "Fuck this printer! It's losing color again!"

Sherry, a fifty-year-old woman with flaming red hair and your typical Midwestern conservative Republican, headed toward a second Encad printer.

"God, Sherry, every single time you touch a printer, it fucks up... Man, oh man... What am I going to do?" Jed returned while shaking his head.

I began inputting a design on my Mac computer when suddenly Lennon, a hip-looking twenty-year-old man with curly brown hair and a goatee approached while pushing up his wire-framed glasses. "So Jed... So like what's up with this weekend? Are you still heading up to Red Rock Canyon?"

Jed then turned toward Jim, a tall jock-like twenty-year-old man with short brown hair and multiple piercings in his eyebrow and ears. "Jim, are you up for Red Rock this weekend?"

Jim answered back, "Yeah probably... But I still have to check it out with my old lady."

"Damn, looks like your old lady has you under her thumb," Jed snickered back.

"Yeah, right... Look who's talking. Like yours doesn't control your ass..." Jim lashed back.

"Fuck you!" Jed returned, embarrassed.

Everyone knew that when Jed was around his wife, he was a quiet, good little boy. No dumb fart or ass jokes were allowed in the company of his wife.

"Well?" Lennon interjected.

"So this Saturday? Right?" Jed asked.

"Yeap..." Jim then confidently returned.

"Okay, then come to my place at ten in the morning," Jed replied, then turned toward me. "Yo, Jerry, do you want to go hiking with us up at Red Rock?"

"Yeah, but I'll have to ask Marvin."

"Don't ask that little weasel... Ask Danny!" Jim blurted out.

"Yeah... Fuck little Hitler," I returned, then shouted toward Danny. "Hey, Danny... Could I get off this Saturday?"

"I don't think that'll be a problem... It's getting slow. Just give me a request form, and I'll sign it."

"Thanks!" I gratefully replied. After walking back to my work station, I turned toward Jed and Jim, "Danny gave me the okay..."

"Yeah, we heard, so why don't you come to my place at ten. We'll be taking off shortly after that..."

"All right, ten... I'll be there..."

CHAPTER 3

BIRDS OF A FEATHER MAY FLOCK TOGETHER, OR DO THEY?

It was eight o'clock in the morning when my alarm went off. I smacked the doze button, hoping to catch ten more minutes of shut-eye.

Looking around my apartment, you would've thought that I just moved in. Most of my things were still in their boxes. I've been living here for almost a year now, but time just flew by. My place was a mess. Besides the boxes of papers and things all over my den, my bathroom counter was full of dried soap, whiskers, and cat hair. The carpet in my den was also full of cat hair. Every single week, I would vacuum the carpets and clean the bathroom, but a week later, I still had same old shit—cat hair on the carpet along with soap scum and whiskers in the sink. Yeah, that's right. What I really needed was a fucking maid.

BEEP!!! BEEEPPP!!!! BBBBEEEEPPPP!!!

I looked at my alarm clock. Just as I was about to turn off the alarm, it went off by itself. It was now 8:10.

Suddenly, my stereo went on by itself, and the sounds of Schumann's Piano Concerto in A-minor, op. 54: *Intermezzo Andantino grazioso* engulfed my apartment. "Great, now I've got the walking spirits of the dead choosing my music." Guess he or she wasn't a Mozart or Beethoven fan.

Well, I did get a whole ten minutes of sleep, and now I felt ever so refreshed. Rubbing my eyes, I made way to the bathroom, where I began the common ritual of a cold morning shower. Well, not that cold. I didn't want to shrink my gonads. After showering, I placed my "eyes" in—my contact lenses. Now I could see everything ever so clearly. You know, like the song. Well, anyway, I threw on some baggy jeans and a T-shirt. Though I was wearing tennis shoes, I grabbed my Nike hiking shoes just in case.

My stomach began to gurgle. I was starving like a Marvin, so I hopped into my white pickup truck and headed up the street to Steinman's, the bagel place. I loved their "everything" bagel especially with lox, capers, and cream cheese. "MMMMmmm!"

As I left Steinman's, I belched. "That was really good. MMmm..." Nothing was better than lox and cream cheese on a bagel with onions and capers. And that "everything" bagel had everything on it, like poppy seeds, garlic, and onions. You name it, and it had it. And that's why they called it an "everything" bagel. Dah!

I began heading north on Decatur Street toward Jed's place, which was in the northwest part of Las Vegas. After about a forty-minute drive, I had reached Jed's house, which was a typical two-story beige suburban tract home that stuck out from the rest of his neighborhood because of its thick green front lawn.

Jed had poured a serious load of fertilizer—and not the shitty kind either like steer manure, but ammonium sulfate. As I neared, everyone was just hanging outside. Jethro, a small, slender thirty-year-old man with a genuine beer belly was standing in front, sucking up his "brew." You could swear that he was from the Ozarks the way he would talk and act, but he really was from Portland, Oregon. That is, if you could believe that.

"Hey, Fletcher, park here!" Jed burped out while pointing to the driveway. After pulling onto the driveway, I slid on my hiking shoes.

Jed and Jethro approached my truck. "Damn there, boy. Looks like they did a good job in fixin' your truck," Jethro replied while scratching his head, as he continued to check out the front end of my truck. A couple weeks ago, in the early-morning hour, I had smacked into a post that hung out off to the side of the facility where I work.

"Yeah, they sure did." While locking my truck, I replied, mimicking Jethro, "Well, then there... I guess... I reckon... They damn there did a good job fixin' my truck..."

After giggling in response to my imitation, Jethro now with a glow in his eye, suddenly wailed out like a hillbilly, "Yee haaa! Let's get goin'!!!"

Within moments, like a bunch of college frat boys heading on a road trip, we all packed into two cars and headed off toward Red Rock Canyon.

CHAPTER 4

HI HO HI HO AND OFF TO HIKE WE GO

As we headed south on Rampart, I visually absorbed the view of the mystical mountainous terrain majestically containing the valley in which Las Vegas resided.

It was funny how Nevada can be so uncreative... For example, to the immediate right was Lone Mountain, a mountain named for being alone and separated from the rest of the terrain. And then there was Red Rock Canyon, which was southwest, named for... You guessed it... It had red rock. But what I couldn't comprehend was why in Sam's hell would this town be called Las Vegas, which means meadows, when the only thing here that resembles a meadow was golf courses and man-made landscapes unless Las Vegas was a metaphor for the meadow of money. And there was plenty of that.

Have you ever seen the casinos here? Well, if you haven't, imagine thousands of mesmerized people sitting in front of gaming tables and slot machines pouring their hard-earned cash to the dealers or machines in the hope that they will hit the "big one." I once heard that Las Vegas was all that was bad about America. Maybe it was. But one thing was for sure, Las Vegas was the hyperbole of dreams. "To start over... To make it rich..." Very few do. But most could start all over.

This city may be the mirage of hope. And I guess that maybe that's why it's green in the desert. But people do need their dreams and their hope. Without hope and without dreams, people would just wither away like decay on a rock waiting to be blown away. So Las Vegas was very much the mirage of hope and the oasis of dreams.

When I looked at the mountains of Red Rock, the multi-reds and oranges would literally come off like a canvas of a great master's painting. It was simply amazing how these mountains of red set themselves apart from their brethren of yellows and browns. One could imagine the natives feeling the holiness within these mountains. It was truly God's real cathedral. As we approached, I felt the sudden calm within the crimson canyon.

While cruising in Jim's silver high-performance Pontiac Trans Am, we were listening to Rage Against the Machine, which created the paradox between the benevolent surroundings and rebellious sounds of music, and so we entered Red Rock Canyon.

Fifteen minutes later, we pulled up before a trail which would lead into Ice Box Canyon. Yeah, you guessed it... It was named Ice Box Canyon for being the coldest canyon in Red Rock.

As we exited the cars, Keyshawn enthusiastically proclaimed, "Looks cool!" Now, Keyshawn was something of a torn individual!. He was the product of the Vietnam War—a war child. His father was an African American, the politically correct name for black, who fought in the Vietnam War and subsequently died shortly after like so many from the exposure to Agent Orange, so he was basically raised by his Vietnamese mother. There was a deep sense of anger within him that would sometimes lash out at odd times. Keyshawn was angry toward his circumstances or the cards of life that he was dealt, but who could truly blame him? It was a funny thing, though, because we would shoot the shit at one another with our latest banter of sarcasm, and no one understood that we were really good friends under this banter, but that was a product of the Midwestern white culture. Since I grew up in Los Angeles, I was exposed to a lot of ethnic cultures, including Black and Hispanic, so I could relate more universally.

"I hear there's a stream and several pools up in this canyon," Jed said.

Lennon replied, "Sounds rad to me." Lennon was altogether an individual with his own quiet idiosyncrasies. He basically would keep to himself unless he was directed with conversation. Lennon was definitely the computer geek, but an artist as well. Though he was born with a silver spoon in his mouth, he worked to keep himself from the depths of boredom. But if you had a question about the use of a program or file, he would emphatically help and answer any question. But altogether like I said before, being the introvert, he basically kept to himself.

"Well, are we goin' to hike or what?" Jethro burped while rubbing his belly and then crushed his empty beer can against his forehead. Well,

Jethro's crude behavior tells you everything about him. Simply put, he doesn't give a flying fuck about what he says or does. We definitely had problems with him in the shop. For instance, there was this one time when an attractive Hispanic saleswomen was at my computer station, where I was discussing with her the possible designs for a show, and from my cubicle, we heard Jethro yell out, "Boy, what a sweet ass... I'd love to squeeze my wienie in her buns!" Hell, upon hearing that, the saleswoman was certainly pissed off, because she certainly wanted to kick his ass, but she refrained. And instead, I spoke with Danny, and of course, he discreetly dealt with Jethro's behavior. But that didn't last long, because it wasn't long after that incident that he was caught "perving" on a secretary in the administration area. And again, though he was disciplined, several months later, he was back at it again... Well, that said, you have the basic idea, which wasn't much when it came to Good Ol' Jethro.

"Dude, you've been drinking in my car! You fucking idiot! What if I was pulled over!" Jim lashed out.

Jethro, with a stupid grin, just smiled back.

And just then I didn't know what came over me, but without a word, I began heading up the trail.

"Hey, Jerry, hold on! Wait for us!" Jed shouted. Ignoring Jed, I continued at quick a pace while being entranced by the magical surroundings.

From below, I suddenly heard the trickle of a small creek while entering into the mouth of the canyon. Though back at the cars, my friends were yelling for me. The sounds of nature would fade in as they faded out. You could hear the chirping of life echoing across the canyon. The small world of the crickets would play their music to their rhythmic beat, and every now and then, I would hear the flutter of wings from a distant chirping bird.

With every step, I would slowly ascend. The flat sandy terrain slowly evolved into a clutter of white rocks and boulders. The terrain quickly turned from desert to temperate. Within what seemed like moments, but were numerous minutes, I reached the creek. Looking up, I became suddenly aware of the changing sky. Out of nowhere, dark clouds began to cross. Suddenly, I heard a shrieking sound. A bird glided across the canyon. There was a sudden mist in the air, but there was no rain.

Leaning down, I placed my palms into the cooling water of the creek then refreshingly wiped my brow. I crawled over large boulders within the creek, not paying any attention if I was on the trail or not. No matter, I just followed the path which I was compelled to follow. Like a spiritual magnet, this silent force continued to pull me toward some destined path. With every step, the desire became stronger. The canyon was like my "Jonah's whale."

While gazing up, I could see the high scaling rock cliffs that surrounded the canyon valley. The sky had then suddenly opened up and a streak of sunlight had broken through. The scenery could have been in a painting by Monet or Renoir.

As I continued on this path along the flowing stream, deja vu began to set in. The surroundings seemed so comfortable, as if there was a belonging.

Up above, there was again a sudden movement of clouds and a small mist began to caress my face.

I took a momentary stop to absorb my surroundings while swigging from my bottled water. A gentle breeze crossed my arms. Goose bumps emerged. I pulled off my sweatshirt, wrapping it around my waist as small birds fluttered by. A lizard then ran into a small bush.

While sitting on a rock and eating its nutty morsel, a small squirrel focused on my approach. As I neared, the squirrel dashed up a lone ponderosa pine. I smiled at the squirrel that was now safely sitting on a branch keeping guard of my presence.

While now sitting on the boulder adjacent to the lone ponderosa, I began to chew on my Power Bar. Still my focus was to continue on my journey, so after quickly gobbling up my Power Bar, I again continued my ascent, climbing over the massive boulders toward my destination.

Down below...

"Where the fuck is he?! That dickhead! What the hell is his fucking problem?!" Jed cursed as they all continued walking along the path.

"Don't worry. We'll catch up to him. He's probably waiting at the falls..." Lennon confidently replied.

"Damn that Jerry... Sometimes he can be so... so fucking anti-social," Jed again lashed out.

"Leave him alone, maybe he just needed some space," Jim blurted out.

Jim was your typical working stiff. He would work hard then head to the nearest bar and just drink to pass time. Life to him was work then party and not much else. Jim was the tough guy who was always getting into bar fights. Sometimes he would come into the shop with cuts and bruises all over his face, and Jed would tease the shit out of him, saying that he probably got beat up by his "old lady." But Jim would always blow him off or say something that Jed had no idea how to answer back. So that was Jim, your basic nuts-and-bolts type of guy.

Keyshawn sarcastically replied, "Knowing him... He's doing the Bruce Lee thing. Mr. Tao is probably meditating sitting on a rock next to a waterfall like the 'Kung Fu man.'"

Up along a cliff edge with my back to a massive boulder, while looking straight ahead, I inched my way toward the sound of running water. I hesitantly looked down below. There was a pool of water at my feet. Reaching to my left, I realized that the edge had opened into an awaiting granite landing. The mist continued to cleanse my face as I began to perch down. A small bird flew from one side of the pool to the other. I was at the very end or perhaps the beginning of the canyon. From above, the gentle falls was filling its contents into the awaiting pool, creating a genuine serenity. I felt so relaxed.

While sitting down next to the falls, I closed my eyes allowing thoughts to seemingly and yet mystically flow away. My mind began to enter an area of non-thought while a breeze continued to rhythmically brush my face. My mind began to feel the essence of the trickling water, becoming or rather creating a sudden oneness with my surroundings. Time seem to stand still.

Jed, Jethro, Keyshawn, Jim, and Lennon had suddenly reached the lone ponderosa. The same squirrel sitting on its secured branch observed the approaching men.

They looked at the large white boulders and Jed informed them, "Just beyond these boulders is a waterfall and small pool of water. Fletcher must be there. And when I get there, I'm going to kick his fucking ass."

Jim laughed, "Yeah right. You're going to kick Jerry's ass like I got monkeys flying out of my butt."

Jed chuckled back, "Is that what's coming out of your ass? I just thought that you had brown junk in your trunk. And dude, it's killing the very air that I breathe."

"Whatever..." Jim sighed.

Suddenly, Jed had a stupid grin on his face.

"Oh, no! You fucking asshole! What are you, sphincter-man?!" Keyshawn lashed out as he climbed up the boulder just behind Jed. "You couldn't have just waited until now to blow your fucking fart in my face."

Jed just smiled after reaching the top of the boulder.

From the distance above, I could hear a humming sound, but I refrained from looking up, still keeping my eyes closed. The air seemed to be a converting from cool to warm air and back, but the granite landing that I was sitting on remained cool as Mother Earth. The wetness turned to vapor on my cheeks from the misty air.

Suddenly, I could hear a flock of birds encircling above. The sky felt like it was opening up with a glowing rainbow-like light. A warmth of sunshine felt like it was piercing through the canyon top. My body began to get goose bumps. A tingling sensation began to develop. The light above now felt brighter and brighter with every passing moment. The wind began to swirl. The warm brilliant light and the whirling wind were now but one. The whirlwind began spinning faster and faster. Like a tornado, the mystical whirlwind began to engulf me. I tightly clenched my eyes and mouth shut. My body was suddenly elevated from the granite floor. My consciousness and body began losing their equilibrium. The recurrent spinning of the whirlwind was twirling me like Dorothy's house in *The Wizard of Oz*. I felt like I was caught in some kind of cosmic tunnel.

My mind... My body... My consciousness began to ascend. Ascending to what seemed like no end. I temporarily opened my eyes, and all I could see were shooting stars like I was caught in some kind of Philadelphia Experiment of spatial dimensions. Again I closed my eyes tightly, feeling the effects of the whirlwind as I continued and continued to ascend. Again ascending what seemed to be no end. Ascending... Ascending... Ascending...

The gang finally reached the narrow path along the cliffs. They could hear the flow from the small waterfall. As they inched now along the edge of the cliff, Jed yelled out, "Hey, Fletcher!!!" *Tcher!!! Tcher!!! Tcher!!!* His voice echoed down the canyon.

They continued their crawling ascent along the cliffs until they finally reached the majestic pool and the serene waterfall. All was tranquil.

There was a moment of silence and suddenly out of nowhere, Lennon broke the ice. "What a cool place."

"Yeah it's really cool. But where's Jerry?" Jed replied, surprised.

The landing adjacent the falls was now vacant. I, Jerry, was gone, and in bewilderment, they all stared in their own awe.

CHAPTER 5

BEAM ME UP!

II Kings 2:11   As they kept on walking and talking, a fiery chariot with fiery horses suddenly appeared and separated one from the other: and Elijah went up to heaven in a whirlwind.

Still spinning within the illuminating whirlwind, I felt a sudden slow descent. The swarming warm, golden light began to evolve into a brilliant but intense blue light. During my descent, there was a perpetual numbing of my body and mind like a deep intoxicating slumber of the "Raven's opiate." So I began to fade away into what seemed like a deep, very deep sleep.

Out of what seemed like if not days then hours, I stretched and yawned, now awakened from an apparently long, deep sleep. My eyes slowly opened. Still feeling groggy and my equilibrium still not all there, I took in my immediate surroundings and then realized that I was standing on some kind of a crystal-like platform which was enclosed with enormous crystals of gold, blue, green, and purple which surrounded the platform.

Within moments, a large crystal retracted, allowing me now a full view of my immediate surroundings. It was so surreal that my perspective of reality became distorted.

Though my equilibrium and my mind became more balanced, my body was still tingling with a new sensation as the numbing slowly subsided. I felt as though my blood was beginning to flow throughout my body. A newfound awareness began to emerge. But my first thought was... *Is this a dream?* My surroundings and circumstances could be analyzed by thought, but my feelings reflected an unusual comfort with my immediate environment. Perhaps I was dreaming or I was having what some might call an out of body experience, but nonetheless, there was no immediate fear of my surroundings and I felt a sense of ease and security for whatever reason.

From the distance, a tall figure slowly neared. Though I noticed that I could freely leave the crystallized chamber, I waited with curiosity as the approaching figure's features came into my focus.

The figure seemed to be gliding, but when I looked down, I realized that this was just illusionary, for whatever reason. Perhaps it was just the surrealism of my dream. I suddenly looked up, and a tall platinum blonde angelic man with large piercing blue eyes now stood before me. His skin had an almost illuminating golden glow while his face was strikingly chiseled like that of a stone head of an Adonis Greek god, while towering to what seemed to be at least six-feet-ten.

At the moment, I thought at first that perhaps he was some kind of spiritual guide. Maybe during my present out of body experience, he was going to lead me through my journey in this spiritual realm.

The tall man suddenly, while holding both his palms up toward me with his fingers spreading open forming a two-finger "V" proclaimed, "Kadosh! Kadosh! Kadosh! Adonai svahot!"

"Kadash, Kadash, Kadash," I returned, trying to mimic him, thinking that this meant some kind of hello. I then mumbled to myself, "Whatever that means?"

The tall man smiled at my attempt and in a deep voice, greeted, "Wel... Welcome... For I am Yoshu'ah..."

Still not sure if I was in a surreal dream while questioning my present reality, I asked, "Who, rather... Where? Could... Could you tell me where am I? Or is this just all part of my dream?"

The tall man pointed toward a viewer window which was surrounded by clear crystals. Through the window, Lake Mead came into view. "Wow, Lake Mead... That's cool. So I must be like hovering over Lake Mead in this out of body experience."

Yoshu'ah sighed at my lack of awareness and then replied, "We are one hundred and ten meters above the lake."

"So this is Lake Mead?" I naively asked.

"Ken... Yes..."

21

"So am I dreaming all this? Am I in some kind of a spaceship? And I suppose you're aliens? Man, I've been watching too much *Star Trek*. So are you like Vulcans or something?" Then I thought that was a dumb-ass question.

Yoshu'ah chuckled reading my thoughts and then replied, "Yes that was. And yes, you are in a starship."

I thought, "Wow! What a fucking dream. All I needed was some kind of melting clocks like one of those Dali paintings and I was set. I guess this is what happens when you drop too much acid during your youth. Damn, I'm going to have to remember to write all this shit down."

"You're not having a dream." Again after reading my thoughts, Yoshu'ah shook his head and smiled at my unanticipated naiveté.

"Yeah right," I sarcastically replied.

"No, this is not a dream. Here." Yoshu'ah placed a white crystal in my hand. The crystal suddenly changed from white to a glowing blue. A sudden ice cold sensation rushed through my hand, dropping the crystal.

After pulling my hand away, a deep impression remained on my palm from the crystal. This certainly was not a dream. But come on? Aliens? Starships? Was I caught in some sort of *X-Files* reality. No. This was fucking real and this wasn't no fucking dream. My distorted sense of reality was now accepting what was real.

I looked at my palm and could still see the deep impression from the crystal left on my hand. It was like the pinch that one would give oneself to realize that the feeling of pain never lies. This was no lie. This wasn't any fantasy. This was real. But with the coming to terms with my reality, I still felt a sense of comfort with no fear of any kind. Hell, he didn't look like he was going to probe me. I assumed that he could've done that a long time ago. And he surely didn't seem like he was going to dissect me. So I wondered what he really wanted from me. What would an alien want with me?

And like I said before, though it was strange what was happening around me, I still felt at ease. Even as we walked along the multicolored titanium corridor with their rows of crystal-framed windows, the tall alien had a loving calmness of a divine holy man.

I then introduced myself, "Oh, by the way, I'm..."

Yoshu'ah interrupted. "Jerry... Jerry Fletcher."

"Damn! What are you, psychic or something?"

"No... Just something..."

While staring at the panoramic view of Lake Mead, I asked, "So if we're hovering above Lake Mead, then why aren't we visible?"

He returned, "The starship is cloaked."

"Cloaked? Like *Star Trek*?"

He replied but in a more pompous tone, "*Star Trek?* Oh, yes, of course, *Star Trek*. You're referring to Gene Roddenberry's entertainment program. He certainly did learn something during his stay with us."

"He was on your starship?"

"Yes... You might say that he was inspired by his experience with us."

"Wow. The cloaking... The transport room... And the Vulcan hand gesture... It all makes sense..."

After reaching the end of the corridor, I stopped and asked, "So why did you transport me here?"

"Pahm, Atah tavi'n... Later, you'll understand why. Here..." Yoshu'ah replied as we entered an elevator.

As he stepped in the elevator, I suddenly realized that though his long, white-tailed coat which of course matched his white apparel, was what oddly seemed being worn backwards. I mean the fucking buttons were on the back. I wondered, "How the hell could he possibly put on his coat if the fucking buttons were on the back?"

And suddenly as if he were reading my mind, he laughed, "Like this." And Yoshu'ah's double-jointed arms reversed themselves, reaching his back. It was all so weird. It almost hurt seeing him perform his contortionism.

Moments later, after the elevator door slid closed, we suddenly began moving upward.

The door suddenly opened and I was at awe seeing the multi-level flight deck with several aliens of all different appearances appearing to be gliding across the deck, while other aliens were seated at their crystallized monitors. Some of the aliens looked similar to Yoshu'ah's race, tall and very slender but still humanoid, but what caught my attention was a select few that looked like children with big heads.

Yoshu'ah noticed me staring at the big-headed children and responded, "They are Cherobi'm. They are childlike, yet quite powerful. With a single thought, they could provide enough energy to keep all of California's utilities running for a day."

We sat at one end of the bridge. I could hear the other aliens speaking in a very guttural language. It was quite similar to something I've heard before. I asked, "What language are they speaking?"

"Speaking... Oh, they are speaking Evri, Hebrew."

"What? Hebrew? So are you Jewish aliens?"

Yoshuah chuckled and then replied, "I see... You'll need to understand the truth about many things."

"Many things? Like what? You being Jewish?"

Yosu'ah chuckled, "No, Jerry no... We're not Jewish aliens. We are Star souls. All of us here on this starship come from many different star systems. There are those that have come from the Orion star system while others like myself are from the Pleaidian star system. We've visited the Earth plane fairly often."

"Often? How often?"

"For over fifty thousand earth years.... We've been continually in contact directly with some Earth souls as well as the Star souls that reside on planet Earth."

"Star souls? Earth souls? I don't understand?"

"Not all people on Earth are Earth souls, in other words, are Earth originate. Some are alien souls or what would be more correctly called Star

24

souls, but are inside the physical bodies of humans. Things are not always what they seem. Like at yourself, for instance. Your soul is not originally from Earth, but from the Orion star system. There are multiples of people who are actually alien souls or rather Star souls. These individuals are usually clairvoyant, creative, and yet sometimes very nonconforming or antisocial. Some are artists, scientists, philosophers, prophets, and so on. Some are thought to be crazy. Others were considered geniuses or prophets in their own right. Some earthlings even had the misunderstanding that these Star souls were perhaps gods or that their offspring were son of gods or God."

"So are you saying that people like Einstein, Picasso, Buddha, Socrates, Jesus, and even Moses were aliens?"

"No... Physically they were in human form, but their souls were not from Earth or Earth originate."

"So you're saying that I'm a fucking alien?"

"No and yes... Like I said before... Your physical form is of Earth but your soul, your spirit is from the Orion complex."

"I understand that now, but why are you or rather how is it that you're speaking Hebrew?"

"Now regarding Evri, the language that we speak was taught to Avraham. This tongue was taught to his children and so on. The Egyptians spoke a similar dialect or language, which we also speak. They too had learned that tongue from us thousands of Earth years ago, but we speak in many tongues and many dialects. At times when we feel lazy, we will communicate by thought. What you would call telepathy."

I tried to soak in what Yoshu'ah was trying to tell me, but it all sounded too easily formulated. Hebrew? Aliens, or rather Star souls? Oh, come on. It seemed all too convenient, like a damn comic book. All I needed was Flash Gordon, and I'd be set. Oh yeah, he speaks Hebrew, so it would have to be "Flash Moshe" right?

I critically lashed back, "Wait a minute! Hold on, buster... You're telling me that I'm an alien or a Star soul and you speak Hebrew and so on and so on. This seems just a little too far-fetched."

Yoshu'ah, surprised by sudden sarcasm, "I'm sorry, but I thought that you understood by now."

"What? That I'm an alien? Oh, come on now. Give me a fuckin' break."

After Yoshu'ah sat down, I followed suit, and then he tried to explain, "Haven't you ever wondered why you've always felt like a complete stranger on the Earth plane? How do you feel here in our starship?"

"Fine, I guess."

"Do you feel a sense of belonging?"

"Well, yes. As matter of fact I feel real relaxed... Like at..."

"Home."

"Yeah, home."

"Like I said before, your soul is from the Orion Star complex. In fact, come to think of it, you're from the very same planet that Eli'ahu, or rather Elijah is from."

"Elijah? You mean Elijah from the Bible? So he was an alien too?"

"Was, no. Is. He is a Star soul. A Star soul in a human's body much like yourself."

"I can't believe it... So he wasn't taken by a fiery chariot in a whirlwind into the sky?"

"No, like you, he was transported or as you would call it, 'beamed up.' Well, almost like you." Yoshu'ah chuckled.

"So why hasn't anybody known about this? About you?"

"Come on, Jerry... They can't... They couldn't accept what they do not understand. So we merely expanded what they had already known or believed to be the apparent truth... At first, they thought that we were angels. Angels sent from G-d. No, we're not Archangels. But we are of the LIGHT. G-d's LIGHT. So, in their perspective, we were angels."

"So there aren't any angels? It's all fairy tale bullshit?"

"Jerry, Jerry, Jerry... I'll explain and then perhaps you'll have a better understanding and see the light. There certainly are angels, souls on the non-physical plane that unconsciously work in the LIGHT."

"So why am I here? What does all this alien angel crap have to do with me?"

"You are an integral part of what is about to manifest. Your destiny to come to Las Vegas was planned. Your many tribulations and challenges were an essence of your true path that was not to be diverted. You are not a simple pawn on the chessboard, but a major part of what is destined to unfold. I'll clarify the whole picture of the universe, so that you'll have clearer understanding. You see, Jerry... There are two forces within the universe. There is LIGHT. And there is DARK. And G-d created both with equal measure. For LIGHT defines DARK, and DARK defines LIGHT."

"Light? Dark? Angels? What does this all have to do with me?"

"Jerry, let me paint the whole picture and then it will become clear. Now, like I said, angels do not have choice. But all souls do, no matter what they may think. We all choose our paths and the results of our actions. We can choose the path of LIGHT or the path of DARK. Though there are angels of the LIGHT, there also exists what some call 'fallen' angels or angels of the DARK. And like I said before... neither can choose. Now, just as the humans reach out for guidance from angels, so do we reach out to the angels of the LIGHT. But understand this, that there are those who equally choose DARK, and so doing, they are guided by the DARK angels. We have been involved in the war for Earth's plane for several thousand Earth years. The Earth souls have often confused our actions as well as the actions from the Star souls who follow the DARK. For some, they may think that there is gray and not all is just DARK and LIGHT. To some extent there is, but this phenomenon resides more within each individual. But at present, there is a clear line that has been present on the earth plane whether those choose to accept it or not. There is the LIGHT, and there is the DARK. But very often, the Earth souls thought that the unexplained events were carried out by angels, even though these were truly actions manifested by Star souls, or as you called us, 'aliens.'"

"So you mean, when... when Moses parted the Red Sea, this was really done by you folks?"

"Exactly, here look for yourself."

Suddenly, a monitor resembling a thin liquid aquarium levitated vertically, appearing in front us. And like watching a movie on a television screen, I began watching history in the making.

On the monitor, thousands of Hebrew nomads huddled up at the edge of a cliff as a pounding spray was thrusting up from the adjacent sea. On a distant approach were hundreds of ancient Egyptian soldiers on their racing chariots. As the Egyptians neared, the fear and anxiety was embedded on the faces of the Hebrew nomads. Just as the Egyptians approached the huddled Hebrews, from within the sky came a laser beam which was now continually striking right before the speeding chariots. Several chariots, unable to stop, disintegrated into thin air from the blazing beam which now could be seen actually being emitted from a hovering starship just above a cloud.

Suddenly, a second starship was hovering above the thrashing sea. A massive white light from the hovering starship projected into the sea adjacent to the Hebrew nomads. The sea suddenly opened up, forming a corridor with cliff-like walls of sea, thus creating a path for the Hebrews to cross. The nomads quickly dashed across. But then, after nearly all the Hebrew nomads completed their crossing to the awaiting bank, the fiery beam holding back Pharaoh's army retracted into the sky or rather the starship. The Egyptian warriors raced across, entering the path of the Hebrews. After almost all the Egyptian warriors entered, the massive white light above suddenly turned blue, and like a hungry whale, the massive sea walls collapsed, swallowing the Egyptians into its belly. On the opposite embankment, the Hebrews stood with amazement.

"So... would you like to see more? There were numerous accounts of these so-called miracles."

"All right... What about when Jesus walked on water. You know at the Sea of Galilee."

"Who?"

"Jesus. Jesus Christ."

"Jesus Christ." Yoshu'ah chuckled and replied, "Yeah, you mean Yoshu'ah Me' Natsaret. Well, he was a Star soul much like Moshe, Moses. And like Moses and other Star souls, he had the ability to heal, but the 'walking on water' was created similar to our recreational deck utilizing multiple projections to create a three dimensional visual image. It's similar to the live special effects that are used in creating your motion pictures. Your movies..."

"Okay, but what about the fish that Jesus gave to the people?"

"You mean the replication of edible species... What you call cloning."

"Cloning? How could you clone so fast?"

Yoshu'ah laughed. "Jerry, come now... Replication technology is such a primitive technology."

"Okay what about Jesus's or Yoshu'ah's resurrection?"

"Well, contrary to what Christians believe, he was never resurrected, because he never died on the cross. He was given an anesthesia and was placed in a cave, but when he was to be transported, he suddenly wandered off, still under the effects of his medication. He was finally located and transported, but it was too late. He was already observed by some of his friends wandering around. They naively had thought that he rose from the dead. Funny thing... the human species, sometimes they need to exaggerate and or create what they cannot explain or comprehend. You know the tabernacle, the ark, that the Israelites carried..."

"Yeah..."

"The Israelites thought it was for performing rituals and praying to G-d, but it was actually just a communicator."

"So you're saying all these biblical events that were thought to be of G-d or the angel's actions on his or her behalf were really performed by aliens?"

"I hate to disillusion you in your belief of G-d, but yes. Now Jerry, you're looking at the truth in a negative way. The truth is that G-d and the universe carry their message of love by utilizing our spiritual guides and the angels of the Holy One to lead us to perform these acts. These acts were performed to protect as well as educate and enlighten the Earth souls.

"But like I explained you before... There is a DARK side along with a LIGHT side. There are DARK aliens or DARK Star souls who are guided by their DARK angels to counter our actions. In the universe, for every action, there is a reaction. So for every action toward enlightenment, there will be an equal reaction toward unenlightenment and vice versa.

"For example, Yoshu'ah spoke of love and G-d, which is found in one's heart, but not from a church. The LIGHT that came from his teachings as well other great prophets was twisted and changed by souls of the DARK, thus creating a hierarchy out of the belief in G-d. These DARK souls created the churches, the synagogues, the temples, and mosques. They created these institutions for power to control and enslave the masses. If anyone disagreed with their views, they were tortured and/or killed as would-be heretics.

"Power and manipulation manifested when the spiritualism of G-d was conformed into the lie of institutions—the churches, synagogues, and mosques. The churches, synagogues, and mosques have used religion to manipulate for their power-hungry hierarchies without concern of the truth or G-d's message of love. These institutions were ultimately created by the will of the DARK side. With the help of Star souls of the DARK, these institutions governed the Earth souls, preaching fear and utilizing guilt to control them.

"A funny thing, though... Now, the DARK souls have used the monetary or economic system to control the masses and retain their illusionary power. Have you noticed how corporations are now interwoven with the same governments that were to regulate and oversee them? Churches, corporations, and governments are married to the same covenant of the DARK. When you return, you will become quite aware of this realty happening around you on the Earth plane. You will slowly recognize or remember what I'm telling you. But most important, you will become fully aware of who and what you are. And then through counsel and watch, your destiny will unfold before you. So, my brother... When you return, open your heart, and your eyes shall hear... Open your mind, and your ears will see... Open your soul, and your love will be with thee."

Back at Red Rock Canyon in the mouth of Ice Box Canyon, metro police and reporters were huddled around Jed and the gang like busy bees in a hive. Above, two helicopters continued their circular flight, searching for me while rescue crews below within the canyon continued their relentless search by foot.

Meanwhile, on TV...

"Hello, this is Nina Fernandes at Channel Four News with a live news update... Earlier today, a hiker mysteriously disappeared in Red Rock Canyon. The hiker, Jerry Fletcher, apparently disappeared in Ice Box Canyon... It's been six hours since his disappearance, and rescue teams continue their search... We take you live to Red Rock Canyon, where Kelly Babonivitz is covering the search..." the young, dignified Latina newscaster announced.

From Red Rock Canyon, a "hip," young slender woman with shoulder-length dark brown hair along with the grace of a high fashion model wearing black framed glasses came into view of the monitor and in an English accent explained, "Well, Nina, as you stated... Jerry Fletcher along with his group of friends went on a casual hike in Ice Box Canyon in the Red Rock Canyon Reserve. But apparently, Fletcher broke away from his hiking group and went ahead into the depths of this canyon. When the hikers, his friends, finally reached the end of the trail, Jerry Fletcher was nowhere to be found. And as you can see, the canyon walls are quite steep. Also, at the very end of the path is a small waterfall with a very steep pitch and no way out. The rescuers patiently continue their search. So it remains a mystery..." She stopped and then slowly emphasized, "Where is Jerry Fletcher?"

Jethro and Jed were suddenly approached by Kelly as the camera followed. "Can either of you explain the circumstances of Fletcher's sudden disappearance?"

Jed looked into the camera, "Well, we were hiking and Jerry started dashing ahead of us like a mountain goat and then we lost sight of him..."

Jethro, with his belly popping out like he's ready to give birth, added, "Well, all I can tell ya... As soon as I caught sight of him sitting next to the falls... He just plum there vanished like something in them sci-fi movies."

Kelly looked into the camera with a very determined look and in her cool toned English accent replied, "Interesting. Well, Nina... as you can see the search continues for Jerry Fletcher while his friends remain mystified to his sudden and yet questionable disappearance.

Metro is here to investigate, if in fact, there were other reasons for Fletcher's unexpected and unexplained disappearance. Back to you, Nina..."

While back on the starship's flight deck, Yoshu'ah began introducing me to several other crew members, which included the humanlike aliens along with the strange child-looking ones with the big heads, the "Cherobi'm." Though there were a select few that could've been Yoshu'ah's clone, most were more humanlike. They were generally of a Mulatto blend with their many features originating from several races. But each had that unique glow like Yoshu'ah as if their skin was emitting light.

The Cherobi'm seemed to be always at play. I mean if they weren't kids, they sure acted like they all belonged on a fucking playground. They had such joy and happiness. And unlike the other members of the crew that seemed to glide when they walked, the Cherobi'm instead skipped and danced to their stations. While they were apparently working, they seemed to be just horsing around. I had asked Yoshu'ah about this and he explained that the Cherobi'm are born as children and remain children throughout their physical lives. He further explained that to be a Cherobi'm meant you were truly at the epitome of the spiritual realm, that being a child. So to enter a lifetime of the Cherobi'm, one had to heal so much so that the only frequency vibrating within the soul was the love of a child. That is why one can only enter the gates of the Almighty as a child. This is perhaps why there is the expression that we are all in search of the inner child, because the Cherobi'm are this epitome.

"Damn, I guess people could learn a lot if they just opened their hearts and minds," I thought to myself.

"That's right!" Yoshu'ah returned, smiling. I wasn't used to the concept of his psychic ability to read my thoughts.

It was also strange that though I was exposed to very large amounts of information, I wasn't overwhelmed. This in itself was the real surrealism of my adventure on this starship. I felt like a damn computer that was continually being downloaded and updated both in data and memory.

"Oh yes, I have someone that you should definitely meet," Yoshu'ah continued to say while heading toward the bottom of multi-leveled deck. Suddenly, we approached a very hairy man with thick black hair and beaming blue eyes. The hairy man, still sitting, turned and smiled through his thick, wavy black beard.

"Jerry meet Eli'ahu... Elijah..." Yoshu'ah introduced me to the biblical holy man.

In total amazement, I stuttered, "The Elijah... the Elijah from the Bible... Ah... Oh... Oh... My... My G-d... You're a... alive...."

"V'shalom... Ma shlom'ha..." Elijah replied in a very deep guttural voice.

Yoshu'ah looked at Elijah. Elijah nodded back and then continued, "So how are you enjoying your experience on our starship?"

"Fine... But... But tell me... How is it that you have lived so long?"

Elijah explained, "Young man, time is not linear as you may think. When you travel through space at rates at multiples of the speed of light well... Well, anyway, time is not what you think it is... For example, there are infinite dimensions in the universe, and thus, since time is a dimension, therefore, time is infinitely dimensional... So my time of existence in this physical body could not be calculated correctly by any present earthly means."

"What? Sounds like Einstein's physics to me... But?"

Elijah interrupted while laughing, "Einstein's physics... Well, along with the phenomenon of time, our ability to heal and regenerate living tissue has enabled us to live well beyond a thousand Earth years."

"Wow, that's amazing. And just think of all the Jews who think that you're..."

"I know. I know... That I'm going to come back and never did die. Well, I never did die and I certainly did come back," Elijah sarcastically replied.

Yoshu'ah then changed the subject while holding my shoulder. "Jerry, we've observed you for many years. You have endured many challenges in your present Earth life. You have lived and felt the suffering of Job for ten years, but still, you kept your faith in the Holy One. As a Star soul... a Star soul that has maintained within the path of LIGHT while at all times the DARK has tried to destroy you and divert you from your enlightened path. But still you showed that you have the perseverance to fight another battle. The DARK came in many forms via the IRS, the Franchise Tax Board, the Los Angeles County District Attorney's Office and, of course, your ex-wife... Yet, you persevered... You rose up and submitted yourself to the very will of G-d and the Universe. Through long periods of duration, during your solitude, you still projected your love in the spiritual realm. Your love of G-d and the Universe... This love is the simple tool of the LIGHT. Because of your love of G-d and the universe being true that it is... Like that of Daniel... We transported you here. We felt that you were ready to handle the truth. You needed to know who you really are. You are a Star soul of the LIGHT... A spiritual Warrior... A Warrior of the LIGHT!"

"So what now I'm supposed to be another Jesus or Buddha? How can I possibly change things on Earth? I'm just a simple man."

"You are simple, but one with heart and soul. But you'll have a better understanding after I complete the picture of the chessboard and with this knowledge. You'll comprehend the very situation and circumstances that are about to unfold."

"All right... Explain away..." I replied while leaning back unfolding my arms.

Yoshu'ah stood up and continued, "As I already told you about Yoshu'ah Me' Natsaret, he taught love of G-d and the universe, like all other prophets such as Buddha, Isaiah, Daniel, Joseph, and so on... But the DARK took what was LIGHT and manifested the institutions of religion, creating the hierarchy of power. The Christians in the name of Christ, in the name of religion have slaughtered Jews, Moslems, Indians, Polynesians, and hundreds of other peoples. They rationalized their enslavement and exploitation of their black brothers under the guise of Christ. Jews and Arabs, though are brothers, sons of Abraham, are still fighting over religion. In every segment on Earth, the governments and religious institutions along with the now-powerful corporations are allied to the DARK. Those who have shown LIGHT and that have risen up for the truth have been killed, tortured, or imprisoned. The DARK have used their weapons of ignorance, fear, hatred, and guilt to subdue the souls of Earth to that of a simple drone.

"As I explained before... We've been in a great war with the Star souls of the DARK. These DARK Star souls are from star systems like ourselves. They've been in contact with the Star souls of the DARK on Earth. For thousands of Earth years, they have controlled the status quo of the Earth plane. They have tried to destroy the American Indians, the Jews, and the Buddhist monks of Tibet, and so on... They have tried to extinguish any LIGHT manifesting itself on the Earth plane through destruction of people and their cultures. Though the Earth souls have learned much technology,

34

this technology was utilized, but in a destructive and manipulative manner. Now we have come here in full force to save Earth from being swallowed into the depths of the DARK.

"In the past, every move that brought LIGHT into Earth, the DARK star souls managed to counter with another. But we are here to finally swing the pendulum back to the LIGHT. They are afraid. Very afraid... They are desperate. They will use whatever they can to keep Earth in their DARK hands. When you go back to the Earth plane, you will become aware of the tactics of fear, ignorance, and guilt used by these governments, corporations, and religious institutions for their control. They are attempting to filter information, but that is being countered, because the 'Zsunami' of truth is upon Earth. And the LIGHT will overcome the DARK in the Earth plane. And Earth will become LIGHT forevermore."

I interrupted, "Okay. But why am I here?"

Yoshu'ah, with a grin, replied, "You are like many great warriors of the LIGHT. We have transferred large amounts of information to your DNA within your bones, and later, while on the Earth plane, you like thousands upon thousands of LIGHT warriors, will battle to save the Earth plane, bringing LIGHT unto Earth."

"But why can't you come and directly battle with these DARK entities?"

"As of now, our Angel guides have instructed us not to be directly involved."

"But?"

"But in due time... And in that time... Then... The Angels will have risen." Yoshu'ah then handed me a necklace. "Here."

I took the silver-like necklace with an attached silver-like encased amulet which enclosed ten pearl-like crystals. "Thanks." I gratefully responded.

"These will help ground you and give you energy. They will also confirm to you that this is not a dream or..." He chuckled, "an out of body experience." Yoshu'ah then continued, "When you are transported back to the Earth plane, for the meantime, you will not tell them of us... This is for your protection. Only a select few may be told. Your angelic guides will tell you who you may confide in. At Earth's present time, the Earth souls are bewildered about your disappearance. This notoriety will give you the very opportunity to enlighten the Earth souls. Utilize this opportunity. Now, my brother, you must return." He pointed to a crystal chamber that was at the corner of the flight deck.

After I stepped into the chamber, Yoshu'ah smiled and proclaimed, "Kadosh! Kadosh! Kadosh! Adonai Sva'ot!" He then gave me his two finger "V," his hello, and for now, his good-bye.

And with a smile of a father leaving his son, Yoshu'ah softly replied, "G-d loves you. The Angels and the universe love you. We love you. See you soon, great Warrior of the LIGHT. See you soon..." A tear began to roll down his cheek, and suddenly, mystical speckles of white trailing light began whipping around me like a banding electrical tornado when suddenly I....

CHAPTER 6

EARTHBOUND: TIC TOC... TIC TOC... TIC TOC

While feeling like a spinning funnel of energy with lights flickering all around me, I suddenly materialized right behind Jed and Lennon.

I slowly walked up right behind them and nonchalantly asked, "So what's up?! What's all the commotion?"

Everyone was startled by my sudden appearance, while I continued to act as if nothing was wrong.

"Where the hell have you been?" Jed inquired in a shocked tone.

"Damn there, boy... Where the sam hell did you disappear to?" Jethro added.

I smiled while responding, "What do you mean disappear... Well, here I am... So, like, what's up?"

"Jerry, you fucking vanished. And we've..." Jed lashed out.

"You guys are all fucking crazy! Fucking vanished! Really now... Shit, that weed must've been fuckin' A. Was there some 'shroom in that shit or what? Oh, by the way, do you guys still have some of that shit?" I rudely interrupted.

"Yeah, then why was 'Metro' searching for your lily white ass?" Keyshawn lashed back.

From the distance, reporters and Metro policemen, while working through the crowd, were trying to approach us.

Kelly, with her Rastafarian cameraman, sneaked past Metro and the crowd, and then suddenly stuck her mic in my face. "Jerry Fletcher, where did you suddenly come from?"

"The same place we all come from... our mothers," I sarcastically replied.

"Rescue teams have been searching for you, and then, now, out of nowhere, you just suddenly appear. Can you explain?" Kelly continued her questioning.

"I don't know what all the commotion's about. I just fell asleep at the top of the trail next to the falls... Next thing I knew... I woke up and that's when I heard people talking. So I simply returned back down the trail, and voila. Here I am." I then gazed at my left hand, noticing the deep impression in my palm. I rubbed my palm on my chest, and the impression remained. While rubbing my chest, I realized that I was wearing a silver necklace. After pulling up the attached amulet, I stared at the pearl-like crystals within the silver ornament and smiled.

"What's so funny?" Kelly asked.

"Things."

"Things?"

"Yeah, things... Things aren't always what they seem." I smirked and continued, "It's amazing how we can live in such a fishbowl, unaware what's truly happening around us."

I held my head as fatigue began rushing through my body, creating a sudden disorientation and then said, "I'll explain later. But right now, I'm feeling a little under the weather. I think that I need some shut-eye." I shook my head, still feeling a bit fuzzy, and I turned toward Jed. "Let's head back."

Kelly demanded, "Just one more question... You're telling me that you slept for eight hours, and then you just suddenly, woke up, and headed straight down the canyon without being seen?"

"Eight hours? Yeah, right. I've only been gone... Rather, slept, for about two hours." I returned while showing my watch. "You see, it's noon. That's two hours."

Kelly looked perplexed and softly replied, "Ummm... Mr. Fletcher, its six o'clock." Kelly held up her watch showing that it was actually six o'clock.

I mumbled out but those around me could hear, "Wow... It really is six o'clock. Time really is in one's own perspective."

"What? What the fuck are you talking about?" Jed blurted out in bewilderment.

In awe, everyone just quietly stared at me. Trying to break the sudden silence while beginning to head back to the cars, I yelled out, "Let's go already!" I suddenly turned and added with a smart-alecky chuckle, "Call me! And I'll give you an exclusive."

From behind, suddenly, I was being grabbed by several Metro police officers. A Metro officer then commanded, "Sorry, Fletcher, you're not going anywhere but to the hospital for observation."

The Metro officers, in their abduction, escorted me to an awaiting ambulance. One of the paramedics began checking my pulse and another paramedic maneuvered his pen-light like a pendulum in front of my eyes while I was being strapped down on a gurney. All the while, Kelly with her Rastafarian cameraman, was just behind while following.

"Hey, Newslady! Could you follow me to the hospital?! I don't want these fucking 'S.S. officers' to probe me like I was some kind of Mengele experiment!" I shouted while being rolled into the ambulance.

Kelly reached the ambulance, and while grabbing hold of my hand, she compassionately replied, "Don't worry, I'll be with you."

I smiled flirtatiously, answering back, "You're not so pretentious after all."

She didn't answer as ours eyes met. Time seemed to suddenly stand still while this mutual but sudden fixation occurred. We continued to gaze into each other's eyes.

While still gazing into her big, brown almond eyes, I softly replied, "Wow, you really are beautiful. Even under your glasses, they could never hide your true beauty." I was sort of amazed how the words had simply rolled off my tongue.

Kelly blushed, and then realizing that she was still on camera, reversed back to her stern role, "Mr. Fletcher, you said that you came straight down the trail. How is it possible that no one saw you until you suddenly appeared at the roadside?"

"Follow me! And I'll explain!" I yelled back just before the doors were shut.

The ambulance rushed off heading east toward UMC Medical Center.

Kelly and John, her cameraman, quickly jumped into their van and sped off following the ambulance but with a discreet distance.

CHAPTER 7

THE NEW WORLD ORDER

Tao Te Ching 53-

When rich speculators prosper while farmers lose their land: While government officials spend on weapons instead of cures: when the upper class is extravagant and irresponsible while the poor have nowhere to turn-all this is robbery and Chaos. It is not in keeping with the Tao...

In Seattle, Washington...

The World Trade Organization was holding a session behind closed doors. Several U.S. senators and congressmen along with their European and Asian counterparts were attending the meeting with several world corporate leaders. Surrounding the hotel where the World Trade Organization clandestine policies were being shaped and molded, were rows and rows of riot-geared policemen.

Thousands of demonstrators of every age and ethnicity surrounded these riot police. As the demonstrators approached the front of the hotel, tear gas canisters and rubber bullets began to fly out from gun barrels of the riot police. Hundreds of demonstrators were quickly struck down. Through the murky air, the cries and screams echoed across the city street while the rubber bullets and canisters continued to rain upon the marching protestors.

Through a wave of rubber bullets, the demonstrators bravely rushed toward the police. Bottles and rocks unexpectedly were flung into the air, striking down the officers. Then like a Roman phalanx, the riot police pulled up their shields, skirting off the oncoming debris of bottle and rocks. A wave of riot police, some on foot and some on horseback, then suddenly rushed with their billy clubs in hand and began bashing the faces of demonstrators like piñatas. The bloodied demonstrators like bowling pins quickly fell to their knees, all the while still receiving their malicious beating until they finally collapsed unconscious to the ground.

Within moments, riot police from adjacent streets began combing out the immediate area. They rushed upon any bystander and began thrashing their new unsuspecting victims. Now completely surrounded, the demonstrators began to disperse in every direction for cover under the continual onslaught of rubber bullets. Anyone caught with a camera or camcorder was immediately dealt with.

During the ongoing riots of civil disobedience, in a large conference room of the hotel, a Republican leader, a tall slender man wearing a toupee of pepper, and a world corporate leader, a stout balding man, both stood up before a large group of associates who were sitting along a very large table and were clinging their glasses of bubbling champagne.

The smiling corporate leader declared, "To a New World Order!"

After tapping his glass ever so eloquently, the Republican leader proudly confirmed, "Yes! Here's to a New World! To the future and its New World Order!" And with that the acknowledging audience in unison applauded.

CHAPTER 8

SMILE YOU'RE ON CANDID CAMERA

Dressed in a green hospital gown, I was lying on a hard, cold synthetic bed attached to an M.R.I. unit.

While looking through the glaring light above, the silhouette of a woman leaned over me while humming to herself.

"This is all fucking bullshit!" I cursed out.

The young attendant calmly responded, "Okay Mr. Fletcher... Please remain still. The M.R.I. scan will only take a minute." The attendant now stood behind a control panel as my bed began to slowly enter into the rotating orifice of the M.R.I. Only my head had entered the humming machine.

I lashed out again, "This is really bullshit!"

"Please Mr. Fletcher, please... Remain still..."

Suddenly, the white "Dunkin" donut continued its rotation while I was being scanned. You could still hear the low hum and then a sudden click. It seemed that every layer of my skull and brain was being scrutinized.

Kelly, along with her cameraman, had just entered UMC Medical Center. While leaning over the admissions desk counter, and with the gracious manner of a civil Englishwoman ordering "grey poupon," Kelly asked, "Pardon me... But could you kindly please tell me in which room Jerry Fletcher is located?"

The heavyset administrator started punching away on her computer keyboard, looked up at her monitor, and then said, "He's in room four, four, seventy one."

"Thank you so much," Kelly gratefully replied and then turned toward her cameraman, "John... Are you set up?"

John, the young black cameraman with his Rastafarian long flowing dreads and bright ivories smiled back, "Ya, Kel. Ma camera's in the bag, and Fletcher, ma'an, won't even know a thing."

"Perfect."

While I was waiting in an examining room, a doctor suddenly entered with the scanned pictures of my skull and brain. "Well, Mr. Fletcher... How are we doing today?"

"Fine, as a matter of fact, I feel great so why am I being examined? There's nothing wrong with me!"

"The officers were just concerned, that's all. They just wanted to make sure that you're all right especially after you're little ordeal at Red Rock." The doctor explained while clipping the scanned pictures on the wall light. "Hmmm... No fractures or contusions. Brain looks normal. MMMmmm... Well, there's no evidence of any fracture or trauma to your head."

The doctor scribbled some notes on a report in a file. He then flashed a light across my eyes while looking deep into my eyes and then continued, "Looks fine... Well, Mr. Fletcher, have you experienced any dizziness or a sudden loss of memory?"

"No," I answered.

"That's good... That's good... Have you had any nosebleeds?"

"No."

Then he suddenly looked oddly at my left hand. "Wow, that's an unusual mark..."

"It's just an old childhood wound. A mishap I had with dry ice, and it certainly left an impression on me." I smiled. "Never play with dry ice."

"Okay... Well, nonetheless, you look fine to me, but I want you to contact me if you suddenly do feel any light-headedness or memory loss. And of course, if you have any nosebleeds or hearing loss as well, all right?"

"Yeah, of course..." I returned, playing along with the charade.

"Great." The doctor smiled and immediately exited.

I then quickly began to dress myself. While zipping up my zipper with my back to the door, I suddenly felt the presence of someone in the room.

"Well, my Lord, don't stop on my account," Kelly announced with a small girlish giggle.

I playfully returned, "I'm glad you enjoyed the entertainment. Next time, I'll just have do it on a table for ya, and that way, you could slap me with some of them singles."

Kelly sensually hissed like a snake and then replied, "Oh, how I would most certainly look forward to that..." She licked her lips and continued, "It would be better than a bloody night at Chippendales."

"Gee, I never took you for the voyeur type."

"It's certainly titillating to watch, but I would have to say that I'm more of the participating kind," she teasingly replied.

With a sudden stern look, I questioned, "So what is it that you really want to know?"

"Well, I'd like to ask..."

Cutting her off, I firmly grabbed her arm. "But before I answer any of your questions, I really need your help. Can you sneak me out of this fucking lab experiment?"

Kelly smiled, "Sure, but only if I can get an exclusive with you."

"Of course."

"All right then..." Kelly nodded with a smile, then slowly opened the door and whispered, "John... John..."

John discreetly leaned against the door and quietly replied, "Like, what's up, Kel?"

"We need to sneak him out of here."

"Give me a minute. Two cops are..." The door was suddenly shut, but not all the way, giving Kelly a view down the corridor.

John pulled a camcorder out of his bag while approaching the two Metro officers. "Ma'an, could ya give me a statement regarding the status of Mr. Fletcha?" John asked while pointing the camera in the officers' faces.

Like hams, the two officers smiled into the camera, and then one of the officers answered, "Sorry, but you'll have to get a statement from our lieutenant." They both turned while pointing to an older officer who was walking along the corridor.

The two officers turned back around, and suddenly, John was gone.

The two officers quickly dashed to my examining room.

They opened the door. No one was there.

One yelled out, "Hey, Lieutenant! Fletcher took off!"

"Great! That's really just fucking great!" The lieutenant bellowed back, shaking his head.

During the commotion of my sudden disappearance, a dark-suited man discreetly approached the nurse's counter. Seeing that no one was really paying any attention because of the upheaval, he inconspicuously leaned over the nurse's counter, then removed some papers from a file while placing others in its place.

CHAPTER 9

THE BREAKFAST CLUB

Sunday... 8:00 am....

"Where the hell is Fletcher?!" Marvin screeched out while nervously pacing back and forth in the warehouse.

Linda, a tall woman in her early thirties with a jolly attitude, approached Marvin, and timidly blurted out, "Marvin, didn't you see the news yesterday?"

"What news?"

"Jerry got lost in Red Rock. And according to the news, he slipped on a rock and suffered a concussion. He's probably still in the hospital," Linda explained.

"That's no fucking excuse." Marvin coldly replied while writing on a pad, "No call. No show."

"You're not writing him up, are you?"

"It's none of your damn business." Marvin then blasted out, "Now get back to work!"

"Ah, Marvin. That's why I'm here. To get more work..."

"Oh..." Marvin said, suddenly dumbfounded.

I opened my eyes after my deep sleep.

"Oh man!" I yawned while looking around realizing, "Oh yeah... Kelly took me to her place." My feeling of fatigue now had faded quickly to a state of coherence and focus.

While scanning my immediate surroundings with curiosity, I thought that you can usually tell a lot about a person by their home. Her bedroom was designed in an ancient Egyptian decor. Along with the hieroglyphics, sphinx, and the obelisk, there were statues of cats that were proudly sitting in their royal prone position as if they were guarding each doorway and window opening. I guessed that she wasn't your average cat lover, to say the least. But then again, I mean I love cats, but not to that extent. "My God... They were placed like gods at every doorway and window. Maybe she was superstitious or something.

But while carefully looking at all the Egyptian artifacts, I realized then that it wasn't a superstition, but a powerful and yet benevolent feeling suddenly came to my mind. She must be indeed a very spiritually deep person. I wondered, "What then? Was it all just a façade? Was it all show that she was displaying or was this just my inherent misconception of prejudging her thinking that just because she's a reporter then does that make her inherently superficial?"

While stretching, I suddenly realized that I was bare-ass naked. "Wow, I must've gotten lucky."

The door suddenly opened as I mumbled out, "God, I feel so tired."

Kelly, while opening the curtains, answered, "I hope not... For God's sake, you bloody slept enough."

With a flirtatious smile, I quickly replied, "I guess that last night you just fucking wore the shit out of me."

Trying to counter my playful banter, Kelly sternly returned, "Maybe in your dreams."

"Oh, come on, lover. You know it was good."

"Honey, the only lovemaking you did last night was in your dreams."

"But like they say... 'Dreams can come true.' So then tell me! Why am I here in the nude?"

"Because... Because you... You undressed yourself last night..." Kelly stuttered.

"Ah! Too bad... Because if I did make love with you, I would've definitely remembered."

Kelly then added, "And I would've definitely blacked out the whole bloody nightmare. Hell, I probably would've turned schizophrenic just to deal with such a nightmarish event."

"Your nightmare maybe... But my dream..." I playfully replied.

She quickly lashed back, playing the game, "And that's all it will be... A dream... A fucking dream..." She then flirtatiously smiled.

"Perhaps it was a dream. A wet dream at that... Oops! Because I must've had one this morning... Could you please throw me a towel, so I could clean up my dying 'little Fletchers' that are crawling up my leg."

"You're fucking gross. What did you do?! Wank off in my bed?! Shit! Now, I'm going to have to clean my bloody sheets. You fuckin' asshole! I don't know how I'm going to sleep through a night knowing that you had jerked off in my bed." Kelly then threw me a towel.

I smiled while pretending to wipe myself. "Do you want to save my towel? Perhaps as a souvenir?" I chuckled.

Kelly smacked my leg.

"Hey lover, I was just kidding." I winced out.

While slowly standing up with my towel wrapped around my waist, Kelly just stared at my genitalia like a deer caught in the headlights.

I then looked down. It seemed that things were standing at attention like a testosterone exploding eighteen-year-old boy. I guessed from my celestial experience, my body had become physically morphed like a young stud of my youth. My arms were now quite muscular. In fact, I looked all "cut up." Hell, I had a fucking washboard. And all those sit-ups and crunches never made my stomach look so good. The "Calvin Man" would've made me their spokesmodel. Damn, just a couple of hours in space and I was a whole new man. Along with my more physical attributes, my hair lost any fragments of gray. After blinking, I was afraid that I might lose my contact lenses, but then I realized that I wasn't wearing any. My vision was perfect. "Even better than perfect..." I felt like I was doused into the Fountain of Youth, and voila, I was truly a brand new man, but with a body of an eighteen-year-old. I pondered if it was a result of my special journey or did the aliens—rather the Star souls—have anything to do with my sudden metamorphosis. Was I probed? No. But Yoshu'ah did

49

mention something about them installing some kind of "info" in my DNA. Did they do more than just that? But no matter, I felt fucking great!

Now feeling confidently erect, I sarcastically replied, "What?! Do you like the view or something?"

Pulling out of what seemed to be a sudden daydream, Kelly blushingly turned crimson red realizing that she was staring at my crotch. She then boastfully lashed back, "Oh, really now... Can't you even bloody control yourself, or are you just going to be nothing more than an immature, walking hard-on?"

Damn she got me there. Feeling like the sudden fool, I couldn't think of a damn witty thing to answer back, so I did the next best thing in this type of situation. You know when you look suddenly like some fucking idiot. That is...

Change the fucking subject. "Mmm... I smell something cooking."

"Oh shit! The omelet!" Kelly then dashed out to the kitchen.

I threw on my shirt and pants, and then shortly after followed her into the kitchen.

In her very French style kitchen, there were copper pots and pans dangling over the center island of burners. To the far right was the breakfast nook, which opened to a panoramic view of her backyard and the Las Vegas skyline just below. In the distance, I could see the Luxor Hotel at the far right and the Stratosphere at mid-left. I sat down in front of a place setting. Everything was so organized and spotlessly clean. I thought to myself, "She must be a Virgo."

Kelly smiled as she slid the omelet onto my plate and another onto her plate. I poured the rich, aromatic coffee into her cup and then mine. Feeling like I was in some kind of romantic comedy movie with *Cary Grant and Katharine Hepburn*, I politely asked, "What do like in your coffee? Cream? Sugar?"

While gently pouring the spicy tomato sauce over the two omelets, she responded, "Black, please... Thank you."

I just stared as she grated a thin cover of parmesan cheese on top of my omelet. She was certainly the gourmet. Hell, I would marry her right then and there, if she had asked. She was beautiful and quite witty, plus she could cook too. Hell, yeah! I guessed that sometimes love could be found in a man's heart by way of his stomach. But then marrying, let alone falling in love with her, would only be a pipe dream. I poured some grapefruit juice into the two large goblets. I complimented her. "This is like eating breakfast at The Waldorf. Not that I've ever eaten at or even been to The Waldorf, but I could just imagine that it would be something like this."

"Darling, obviously you've never been in The Waldorf," Kelly smirked while sitting down.

I slowly chewed on a morsel. "MMMmmm... This is really good."

"Thanks. Cooking is one of my many hobbies."

"Well, what are your other hobbies?"

"Music... I love music. Art... And well, I'm sort of a movie freak. I love movies, especially the independent ones... You know... Not the mainstream."

"I love movies too. But there aren't many movie houses that show independents in Las Vegas."

"Yeah, I know what you mean, but that seems to be changing. In fact, there's only one theater over at Sahara and Ft. Apache that shows some independents, and sometimes they show independents at the theater in the Suncoast."

"Do you have any family in Vegas?"

Kelly didn't answer.

"Ah... Bad subject?"

"No. It's just that my grandmother had just passed away three months ago. She was my only family." There was suddenly lull of awkward silence and then Kelly continued, "Well, enough about me. You did promise me an exclusive."

"Yeah I did." I began to explain, "Well, we went to..."

"Not now, after John gets here," Kelly interrupted me and then turned on the television. "And anyway, I need to see the news report."

On the television, the seasoned newscaster continued to announce, "As the Hashemite monarchy government in Jordan tried to crack down on the relentless Palestinian protests in Amman, the Israelis and Palestinians have continued to uphold their cease fire agreement while their intense peace negotiations continued. But to the surprise of the State Department, both Israelis and Palestinians requested that further talks will be done without any foreign diplomats present.

"In Teheran, the Iranian government, while being bombarded with uncontrollable protests within its streets, agreed not to execute an outspoken professor who during a lecture criticized the ruling clergy.

"And in Beijing, thousands of students for a third consecutive day continued their sit-down demonstration, protesting the occupation of Tibet. The Chinese government until now has refrained from making any move toward the protesters.

"And in Mexico, rebel Indian forces seized control of the Yucatan Peninsula. It is believed that the Indian rebels are being backed by both the Costa Rican and Nicaraguan governments. President Halliburton warned that any support for the rebels will be considered a threat both to American interests and American security. And he further declared that if these countries continue their unlawful support of the rebels, then they will be dealt with accordingly.

"And around the world's major cities from Tokyo to London, something that has not been seen since the anti-war protests during the War in Iraq, massive protests against globalization have continued for the second week in a row.

"And on the weather scene, the National Weather Service acknowledged that during last month, though we've experienced unusual weather patterns, the increased flooding in the Midwest along the Mississippi, the sudden high humidity and the de-deserting of southern Nevada, scientists believe that these sudden changes as well as other rampant changes in our weather patterns are the resulting affects of the 'greenhouse effect,' and that sunspots are causing the Earth's sudden increase of earthquakes and volcanic activity.

"And now a message from your local news..."

"Hello, this is Nina Fernandes at Channel Four News with a news update on Jerry Fletcher, the young man lost in Red Rock Canyon this

Saturday. According to a Metro Police report, Jerry Fletcher received a concussion when he had fallen on some boulders while hiking at Red Rock Canyon...”

I hollered out, “This is fucking bullshit!”

Kelly calmly replied, “I know... I know... Sometimes the network will cooperate with Metro in order to score some points, if you know what I mean.”

“Whatever... It’s all fucking bullshit!” With aggravation, I got up and turned off the TV.

“You didn’t have to turn it off. I wanted to see more,” Kelly blared out.

“What, more bullshit? That’s all they ever do on the news... More propaganda and more bullshit...”

Kelly was suddenly quiet. Shit, I suddenly lost my head. She’s probably all pissed off by my ungratefulness. Here’s a news reporter who just saved my ass while I was ragging on the very hand that just saved me.

I apologized. “I’m sorry.”

“Don’t be... There’s a lot crap that’s put out there while all of the real news is being kept shelved. And anyway, you were just bloody speaking your mind,” Kelly surprisingly answered.

“Well, anyway, what did you think?”

“About? About what?”

“About the sudden change in our weather...”

“The strange weather patterns? What? They had something to do with your sudden disappearance?”

“Maybe... But not what you think.”

Kelly looked oddly at me and then just stared at my chest.

“What is it?”

“Wow... That’s an unusual amulet. Are you into Wicca or something?”

The obelisk amulet had silver-like casing that seemed to be almost alive with its colors of the spectrum dancing along with an unusual alternating glow coming from the oval crystals within.

I placed my hand on the amulet while feeling a sudden tingling sensation running through my hand and arm. I answered, "No. This isn't a witch's amulet, and I'm not a witch or a warlock. Is this the sort of interview you want? Because if it is... I'm not going to continue a fucking lame-ass tabloid interview. Got it?!"

"No. No. I only want the..." Suddenly the doorbell rang like gothic chimes of an old church. Kelly immediately got up to get the door. She suddenly turned and in a pleasant voice, said, "Jerry, could you please go to the living room. And I promise no tabloid-like interview."

I smiled, thinking that she was sincere. So while I swaggered into her living room, I thought, "Great... hell's... bells... What should I do? Should I? Or shouldn't I? Should I spill my guts? Come on Jerry, you can do it. Spill your fucking guts. So what should I do? All right, all right, all right... I'll do what I gotta do."

Kelly entered with John, who, with his brightly colored Caribbean shirt, was carrying two large silver cases. He smiled while setting up his camera equipment, setting up the interview in the living room.

Kelly sat across from me.

The living room was decorated in a Mayan/Aztec tone. In the middle of her living room, a large Mayan statue poured sparkling water from her mouth while holding her palms up, which contained flowing vines which were blossoming red and purple flowers. The room had its own unique serenity as I listened to the trickle from the Mayan statue.

"I've traveled the historical globe from ancient Egypt to old Mexico. But where's Montezuma when you need him?" I chuckled.

Kelly smiled, and then while leaning forward asked, "So tell me, Jerry... What really did happen at Red Rock?"

"Well..." I briefly paused and then continued, "According to Metro, I suffered a major blow to my head and was unconscious. And I must've suffered a concussion."

"No, really. Tell me what really happened!"

"You have a nice place..."

"Thanks."

"I feel like I'm spanning the globe in ancient times. Do you have ancient Greece or China?"

Kelly, becoming giddy, replied, "As matter of fact, I do. The dining room is set in Chinese decor. And the landscape in my backyard is a traditional Japanese garden with real carp. Would you like to see?"

"I'd love to."

We casually walked into her backyard, which had a running stream and waterfall that emptied into a pond. There was a small path that led through her lush green landscape of flowering plants, Bodhi trees and exotic statues led us to a wooden bridge which crossed a small stream. As we walked over the bridge, I looked down and could see the masses of multi-colored carp swimming, rushing for a feeding as Kelly began dropping morsels of fish food.

"This is truly breathtaking and yet so serene," I smiled.

"Yeah, I know. I need a place for peace and quiet, especially in my line of work, if you know what I mean."

"Speaking of which... Why did you get into this profession? You seem so down-to-earth. You're not what one would expect."

Kelly quickly replied, "What did you expect? That I'd be your typical pretentious and superficial newswoman? Now don't quote me. Or tell anyone that I said all newswomen are superficial, because they're bloody not. It's just a cold, narcissistic industry. So some of us like me gave up their bloody idealism to conform to..."

"So that's why they all look like they just stepped out of a Mormon church?"

Kelly smirked, "Yeah." She sighed and then continued, "It's funny. You're the first person that has asked me why. Huh... Well, after college, like so many kids, I was quite idealistic. I thought if I became a journalist, I would be able to find the truth and tell the public the truth. But since then... Well, since I came to work in Vegas after my grandmother's accident, the only real news seemed to come from the casinos. The rest is... You already know. Bullshit..." She leaned over and threw another morsel to the hungry fish and continued. "But you can't really bloody blame the media in Vegas for exaggerating or making something more dramatic than it is, because that's all we have."

"Wow. You really take your job seriously."

"Well, don't you?"

"Well, I..."

"Listen, Jerry Fletcher, I'm a passionate person. And I truly care about what I do! Now, enough about me... What about you? You did promise me an exclusive."

"I did... Didn't I..."

"Yeah."

"You know... You know, you are very sexy when you're angry."

"I'm not angry. I just had a very long week, that's all." She then indiscriminately brushed up very close to me.

Trying to comfort her, I causally placed my arm around her shoulder and began gently massaging her neck.

"Mmmm... That feels so good." Kelly suddenly grabbed my hand. "But let's head back to my living room. I think John's set up. Okay?"

"Sure."

After entering back in her living room, I saw that a camera was set on a tripod aimed toward the couch.

As we sat down on the couch, Kelly softly whispered into my ear, "So you think that I'm sexy, huh?"

I smiled back. "Yeah, definitely."

Kelly flirtatiously smiled at my remark and then turned toward John. "Are we ready?"

With his long, flowing braids, John returned, "Yeap. Justa give me your cue when you're ready."

"Great..." Kelly replied then turned toward me with a smile.

She gathered her composure, looking straight into the camera, then nodded and began, "Hello! This is Kelly Babonivitz with Jerry Fletcher... Mr. Fletcher has agreed to give me an exclusive interview regarding his mysterious ordeal this Saturday at Red Rock Canyon. Mr. Fletcher had suddenly vanished during a hike with his friends, and then, suddenly, he appeared out of thin air at the bottom of the canyon. Metro officers escorted Mr. Fletcher into an ambulance, where he was taken to UMC Medical Center for observation. Though his examination showed that he had no abrasions or contusions, there was only speculation that perhaps he may have suffered a severe concussion. Again, there was no concrete evidence that showed that Fletcher suffered from any head injuries whatsoever. So we are here to find out what really happened to Jerry Fletcher.

"Now, before we get into the events that occurred at Red Rock Canyon, Mr. Fletcher..."

I interrupted, "You can call me Jerry."

Kelly smirked and continued, "Okay, Jerry. Could you tell us a little about yourself?"

I scratched my forehead and then answered, "Well, I'm originally from L.A. I came to Las Vegas, like many, for a new beginning. I'm presently working as a graphic artist."

Kelly then added, "Okay. Now, Jerry. What exactly happened at Red Rock Canyon last Saturday?"

I hesitated for a moment and then replied, "Well, how do I explain without sounding like some kind of crazy asshole in a tabloid magazine?"

"Jerry, we just want to know the truth. The public wants to know."

"The public doesn't really care about the real truth. The public is so apathetic."

Kelly responded, "I understand how you feel, but you might be surprised by what the public really wants. The truth, Jerry... The truth..."

I sighed deeply and then explained everything. And I mean everything.

Kelly wanted me to describe the aliens and I did. She wanted me to further describe the starship, but what she became most intrigued was the involvement of these aliens with biblical events or so-called miracles. I felt like I was suddenly giving a talk on one of those nighttime talk shows like *Charlie Rose* or something. When I further explained Yoshu'ah's account of today's events and the dogma of the two alien forces, that being of the Light and Dark fighting each other for Earth and the reason that they are here, that's when the Q & A really got started. I elaborated about the Dark and Light forces within our own world and how Yoshu'ah further informed of the immediate battle or battles that were to come.

To my surprise, Kelly looked at me with an open mind. During the questioning, it seemed as if she was really doing this interview for her own knowledge and not for some news station's benefit. But, no matter, I continued my story while the tape was rolling.

Kelly took a sip of her iced tea while nodding with complete compassion of my whole experience and then replied, "Wow, that was truly amazing... What a story." She took a sip of her drink and continued, "And yet you seem to be so immersed by this massive amount of information..."

"Well, my experience did seem to go by really fast. And yet I was only on the starship for two hours."

"Two hours? You were gone for eight."

"That's whole different thing. But from what was explained to me, we have the misconception that time is linear, having only one dimension, but the real truth is that time is simply infinitely multiple. Though it was only two hours in the earth plane time dimension during my starship experience, eight hours had passed what we considered time on earth."

I sighed and continued, "G-d, I'm just realizing how much I really did learn in such a short time on the starship." I took a sip of my drink and looked at Kelly's seemingly puzzled expression. "Great, now, you're probably thinking that I'm fucking crazy or that I got some kind of fucking tumor in my head or something. Or just maybe, just maybe, I'm just making all this shit up. What do you think, that I'm just looking for attention or something like it's all just a bunch of crap? Right?"

"Well, it all does seem little unbelievable. But then... I saw you... I saw you just..." Kelly suddenly stopped and looked at John. "Cut!"

John turned off the camera and sound. "Kel, you're off."

The doorbell suddenly rang and John left.

Kelly then continued, "I didn't want to continue on tape."

I asked, "Why?"

Kelly didn't respond.

I suddenly lashed out, "You saw me appear. Didn't you?!"

"Yeah, as a matter of fact, I did. I caught sight of you when suddenly you appeared out of thin air. I knew that there was something to this, but until now, I thought you were caught up in some kind of government experiment or something. Living in Las Vegas, weird things are always happening especially when you a have Area Fifty-One nearby."

John walked in and announced, "Kel. Ma'an, like there's two cops at the front door looking for the ma'an."

Kelly turned toward me and requested, "You'd better go into the garden and stay out of sight."

"Why? I didn't do anything."

"Jerry, don't be stupid. They want you quiet and out of the public's eye. Why would they fabricate what happened to you at Red Rock? So get the bloody fuck out of here!"

Without delay, I immediately headed into Kelly's Japanese garden, and after finding a secluded area, while listening to the trickling of water, I sat down and closed my eyes.

Kelly opened the front door. Two plainclothes detectives with very dark suits and dark sunglasses immediately flashed their Metro badges.

One of the detectives inquired, "Ma'am, we're looking for Jerry Fletcher. He apparently disappeared from the UMC Medical Center. And well, he was last seen with you."

Acting puzzled, Kelly responded, "Well, I don't know what to say. I have no idea where he might be."

Both detectives invited themselves in and one asked, "Would it be okay if we just took a look around?"

"Sure... But I haven't seen him since he was taken to the hospital."

The two detectives smirked. "Yeah sure."

CHAPTER 10

HIDE AND SEEK

Kelly kept her composure while the detectives continued with their investigation, more like their exploration.

After the detectives made their rounds throughout her house, while sipping on her cold refreshing glass of ice tea, Kelly asked with a scattered sarcastic tone, "Well, detectives, are you two bloody finished? I do have a lot of work to do, if you don't mind."

Both the detectives suddenly oddly gawked at the camera equipment in living room. The older detective politely asked, "Pardon me, but were you in the middle of an interview?"

"No..." Kelly quickly answered and then continued to sip on her ice tea. The older detective glanced at his partner with a cold glare. The older detective then looked at the half-empty glass of iced tea.

Kelly, realizing the predicament, yelled out, "Hey, John! You forgot to finish your iced tea!"

John responded from the hall, "Iced tea?"

John suddenly entered, and Kelly gave a look. "You forgot your drink."

John looked down, "Oh, ya, ma'an, my drink. So that's where she be." He picked up the glass, gulped down the drink, and replied in a Jamaican accent, "Ahh! ma'an, now that was truly refreshing. Would you two like some, ma'an? It's a special island blend straight from my homeland." He stopped and then smiled, "Ah, ma'an, now don't ya worry none. There's no ganja in this here brew. Ma'an, are ya sure ya wouldn't want some?"

The two detectives then just looked at each other. The older one then replied, "We'll just take a look around in the backyard, and then we'll be out of your hair."

"Take your time, detectives. Just take your bloody time," Kelly returned sarcastically.

The detectives and Kelly entered her Japanese garden. The detectives were suddenly captivated by her illustrious garden. They could still hear the running stream with the momentary splash from the multicolored carp, and they absorbed the view of the large bamboo fountain at one end which would periodically drop its contents into the awaiting mouth of the gentle stream.

"Quite breathtaking... You would think that you were in Kyoto." The younger detective blurted out.

Kelly discreetly looked around for me, but was confused by my sudden and yet mysterious disappearance. She mumbled to herself, "Not again."

The younger detective responded, overhearing Kelly, "What again?"

Quickly thinking, she looked at her pager, "Oh, shit! The fucking station is bloody paging me again."

The older detective smiled while replying, "Well, he's certainly not here, and I've seen enough."

"Enough?" Kelly questioned.

The older detective continued to smile. "Thanks for your time, ma'am." Both detectives quickly left Kelly's home and sped off in their black Lincoln Town Car.

"Ma'an, I hate them cops," John grumbled out.

"They weren't police. They were feds. You know the spooky kind. Cops don't drive black Lincolns, especially in Vegas..."

"So, ma'an like where did our favorite Martian disappear to?"

Kelly scratched her head and with a puzzled look replied, "Who the fuck bloody knows?! Maybe he was beamed up again."

"Girl, I'ma justa gonna kick it in the back and play some vibes."

Kelly just smiled and began contemplating my story.

Within moments, the soft music of a saxophone was soothing out the gentle vibes of some jazz which could be heard throughout the house. Meanwhile, Kelly was stretched out on the couch reading a small book, *The Tao Te Ching*. Legend has it that this book was written by Lao-tzu, years before Confucius's time, and this master left his book, *The Book of the Way* to a soldier who, while standing guard, asked the master how to live his life, but subsequently then Lao-tzu mysteriously disappeared. Kelly flipped a page and read the following passage:

"If a country is governed with tolerance, the people are comfortable and honest. If a country is governed with repression, the people are depressed and crafty.

When the will to power is in charge, the higher the ideals, the lower are the results. Try to make the people happy, and you lay groundwork for misery. Try to make people moral, and you lay the groundwork for vice.

Thus the Master is content to serve by example and not to impose her will. She is pointed, but doesn't pierce Straightforward, but supple Radiant, but easy on the eyes."

Kelly leaned back while mumbling, "I wonder... Maybe... Could this book also been inspired by...? Nah..."

She looked at the book again and then stared intently into the empty space of a daydream glaze when suddenly from behind her, John said, "You don't minda if I flicka on a little of the idiot box, do ya, Kel?!"

Kelly jumped up startled from her deep thoughts. "What?!"

"Oh sorry, Kel... Were you justa sleepin'?"

"No just thinkin'."

"About Jerry, ma'an, or about what he said?" John asked with a small grin.

"About what he said..." Kelley lashed back, camouflaging her apparent denial.

"Girl, are ya sure? Cause, honey, from where I was standin', them sparks were sura flying so high that my eyebrows got singed."

"Ah, fuck you! I was just fascinated by what he bloody said, that's all," Kelly paused and then continued, "but really it seemed so bloody deja vu. Didn't it?"

John smirked and then shook his head with a small giggle.

"What?" Kelly added. "Didn't he? I mean what he was inspiring about?"

"Yeah, ma'an, but I've known ya Kel for a long long time and I know when your startin' to get the love bite."

"Oh, come on... He so fucking bloody immature..."

"Whatever, my dear..." John replied in a girlish English accent, mocking Kelly.

Kelly continued, "But really... He seems so innocent and yet so fucking immature while all in the same time being so... So fucking bloody enlightened..." She sighed, "He's... He's a bloody oxymoron. That's what he is... He's so disgustingly juvenile while all the same being enlightened with the purity of a bloody Buddhist monk. How moronic or rather bloody oxymoronic..."

John flicked on the television.

"Hello, I'm Marcus Harrison with this Channel Four News Update," the news anchorman declared and continued. "In Genoa, Italy, riots have broken out after thousands of demonstrators began protesting the G8, the meeting between the eight largest industrial nations. The demonstrators were protesting against globalization policy, which they believed is an attempt that the G8 is creating economic and ecological policy in the interests of corporations barring any possible democratic representation.

"The outbreak of riots occurred after police fired and killed a teenage boy. During the G8 meeting, after news of the death of the teenager, President Halliburton while addressing his fellow leaders said that it was a shame that the death of the teenager occurred, but it was also sad how the police have had to deal with the demonstrators."

Kelly turned off the television and then headed into her Egyptian bedroom.

While in her master bathroom, which was adjacent to her bedroom, Kelly began singing, "Wild thing, you make my heart sing... You make everything so groovy..."

Kelly turned on her shower. The warm continual spray began hitting the bathtub while Kelly fluttered her way back to her bedroom. She dropped her pants and then removed her blouse, baring all, exposing her breasts. She then gazed into the mirror, admiring her suppleness. While still looking into the mirror, she continued to softly caress her breasts. But then suddenly, there was a loud THUMP!

Kelly, startled, threw on her towel, quickly wrapping her breasts. Again, there was a loud THUMP! Again another THUMP!

Kelly, while listening to the loud THUMPS, followed to its source.

THUMP! THUMP! THUMP!

She briefly stared at sarcophagus, the ancient tomb of a mummy. The THUMP was coming from the sarcophagus. Kelly ever so carefully opened the lid and then jumped up screaming, "AAAaah!!!" as I emerged from the sarcophagus.

After I stepped completely out of the Pharaoh's crypt, Kelly poked me hard on the shoulder. "You fucking son of a bitch! You scared the holy shit out of me!"

"Sorry," I pleaded.

"Sorry? What sorry?" Still pissed off, she admonished, "What the bloody hell were you doing in my bedroom in the first place?!"

Trying to explain, I first stuttered, "Well... I... Umm... I saw the two detectives head out into the garden, so I crawled through the window. Then I found myself in your bedroom. And... but then I heard them, so I thought that they might come here, and I hid in this tomb. After I closed the lid, I suddenly dozed off. And the next thing I know that's when I heard you singing, I woke up. So I tried to open the lid, but fuck! It wouldn't open, so I..."

"I got it. I got it. I get the bloody picture."

"So what did Metro want with me?"

"They weren't cops. They were Feds."

"FBI?"

"Maybe, maybe not, but they were definitely feds."

"So what did they want from me?"

"That's the point. What do you know that they want you so fucking bad? Maybe they are somehow aware that you have been in contact with the aliens? We're going to have to watch what we do and say." Kelly suddenly stopped while pulling my hand, leading me into the bathroom. She then quickly turned on the faucet and continued, "From now on, because they're definitely watching and listening to us right now." With an odd boyish grin, I just stood there admiring Kelly's hot body silhouetted under her towel.

Kelly suddenly whispered, "By the way, knowing the bloody pervert that you are... Did you happen to see me when I was..."

"Naked! Hell, yeah! I'm not dead!" I suddenly looked down, realizing that I had a woody. Damn, I was feeling like I was back at college again. Man was I ever so fucking horny...

"For God's sake, can't you control yourself?!" Kelly sighed.

"I would if I could, but ever since... Well, I feel like..."

"So eight hours on a starship turned you into a fucking bloody horny Buddha man?"

"Well, yeah..." I returned with a smile.

Kelly just shook her head while rolling her eyes back changing the subject. "Tomorrow, we'll think of how to sneak you out of here and what you should do."

I added, "Yeah, when it comes to the government, there's no due process. Hell, they'll just throw your little ass in a discreet closet-like cell and then forget that you ever existed. That is... If you're ever so lucky, and you don't just simply disappear in the many foxholes surrounding Las Vegas in the Nevada desert, and all this in the name of national security."

Kelly sarcastically replied, "Well, if you don't quit your perverted behavior, I'll bury you my fucking self."

"Ah, you know you love me..." I laughed back and Kelly just sighed with a smile.

CHAPTER 11

SPEAK YOUR MIND AND THE REST WILL HAPPEN

I suddenly felt a soft caressing touch across my forehead. Nothing's better than a deep sleep. Again my forehead received the gentle caressing but accompanied with soft gentle lips brushing my ear, "Jerry... Jerry, are you up? Jerry, it's time to wake up. Come on, wake up, Jerry. Wake up," Kelly had whispered sensually into my ear.

I opened my eyes, and while stretching, I yawned. "Aaaaaaah..." After letting out another invigorating yawn while gazing at my immediate surroundings, collecting my thoughts, I suddenly became aware that I was fucking naked again. Oh, come on, once? And now, twice? Have I been sleeping through the experience or what? Hell, I was butt naked in Kelly's bed again.

Assuming the best, I confidently boasted, "It must've been really good, because I don't remember a fucking thing..."

"Real good, huh? Nothing happened last night except for your fucking snoring."

"Are you sure now?"

"Yeah, I'm sure. The only orgy that you had last night was with Rosy Palm and her five lady fingers."

"But I..."

"But what? After you came out of the sarcophagus, you sat on my bed than suddenly collapsed, falling asleep. So being the kind dignified woman that I am, I covered you in my bed. That is, with your clothes on! Got it, Jerry? Nothing bloody happened!"

"So then where did you sleep?"

"On the fucking bloody couch in the living room... And that's the last time I'll do that!"

While I was pulling up my pants, Kelly just stared at my crotch, and I asked, "What are you looking at?"

Kelly sarcastically replied, "I'm not dead, am I..."

"Yeah, I knew it!" I bantered, "I knew it! You probably did do me last night... You must've taken advantage of me when I was most vulnerable..."

"Yeah right, Jerry. I took you like my little bitch." She continued to tease. "And I must've drugged you last night, and then played you like you were my boy toy. And now that your bloody fantasy has finally been fulfilled, if you should be so lucky, we really need to sneak your skanky little ass out of here... And I mean right now..."

Just across a street from Kelly's house, a blue van with white writing along the sides saying, "The Best in the West Carpet Cleaners - Western Carpet Cleaners," suddenly pulled up along the curb. Inside the blue van were two technicians with highly sophisticated audio and video surveillance equipment. Yeap, they weren't your typical carpet cleaners. They were...

Hank, a frail, balding man with wire-framed glasses and long ponytail, wearing a high-tech earphone and mouthpiece asked, "Hey, Bob! Got a fix on audio... How are you on the visual?"

"Okay... We got a lock," a stocky man with neatly trimmed crew-cut replied, who was also wearing a high-tech earphone and mouthpiece. Suddenly, his monitor was on, and he could see Kelly with a black man with long flowing dreads leaving the house and then entering a news van. The van pulled away.

Hank firmly announced, "Zebra-charlie... Zebra-Charlie... The beetle and the butterfly have left the garden. I repeat. The beetle and the butterfly have left the garden. The caterpillar is still in the garden. We still have no visual or audio on the caterpillar!" KIIICH!

From Hank's earphone, "This is Zebra-Charlie. We are tracking the beetle and the butterfly. Maintain your position. I repeat, maintain your position." KIICH! "Out."

From above, a black helicopter was following the news van, which was now heading east on Sahara Boulevard. The van suddenly turned right on Maryland Parkway, heading south toward the university. The van then stopped near the university in front of a coffee house, "Cafe' Roma...," a hip, trendy eclectic coffee house.

In Cafe' Roma, Kelly ordered a double espresso and a cafe' latte while I was busy trying to wipe off the dark brown makeup on my face in the bathroom. Kelly then took the two cups of coffee to the rear of the coffeehouse and while sitting down, said, "Here."

"Thanks." I replied while sipping on my espresso.

Kelly leaned over to a young Hawaiian girl with blue coloring outlining the tips of her raven black hair and two pierced rings protruding from her nose, who was sitting at the next table sipping on her drink while reading a book. Kelly tried to get her attention. "Excuse me."

The hip Hawaiian girl looked up. "What?"

Kelly pleasantly asked, "I'm sorry to disturb you, but could you help me?" Kelly continued and then looked at me. "Sitting over there is Jerry Fletcher. You know the guy that..."

"Was that the dude who was missing at Red Rock last weekend?"

"Yeah that's him," Kelly acknowledged.

They both looked at me again while I was sipping my coffee.

"He's kinda cute. He looks a lot younger in person," the young Hawaiian girl replied.

"Well, anyway... He wants to explain what really happened to him at Red Rock Canyon. But the bloody feds are coming down on him. He really needs to tell his story in public. And well, I thought that maybe the students could help."

"Yeah. Like no problemo."

"This isn't any kind of bullshit government conspiracy theory, but he really..."

Not paying any attention to what Kelly was now saying, the young girl shouted, "Hey Roxy! Could you tell everyone to meet over at the campus quad." While pointing at me, she continued, "Well, Jerry Fletcher is here with some reporter. You know. You know the dude who was lost at Red Rock. Well, like he wants to tell what's up... You know like what really happened to him at Red Rock, but the fuckin' feds are trying to shut his ass."

Roxy, a tall, slender young black girl with neatly braided hair design on her scalp, nodded and then punched away on a cell phone. She closed up her phone after talking on it and then held her palm up while announcing, "In five!"

"Cool." The young Hawaiian girl acknowledged and then turned toward Kelly. "In five minutes... In front of the quad... Okay?"

"Thanks." Kelly smiled.

The young Hawaiian girl smiled at me and then flirtatiously blew me a kiss.

In a 1968 red Ford Mustang with a white convertible top and a clean white interior, John pulled up behind the coffee house.

John entered Cafe Roma's and walked up to our table. He threw the keys on the table and proclaimed, "Kel, ya sure have one fine set of wheels."

Kelly smiled, "John, you always have such perfect timing. We're about to shoot at the university. Oh, by the way, do want something to drink?"

He replied with a gleaming grin, "Yeah, how about some of that iced tea. But, ma'an, make it green this time." John then smirked.

Kelly ordered the iced tea, and within moments brought the iced tea to John.

"Thanks." John gulped down his green tea like no tomorrow and asked, "So Kel, where are we goin' to set up?"

"At the university's quad."

"Shouldn't we go now?" I added.

"Yeah." And then Kelly turned towards me, "Are you up for this, Jerry?" Through the café's window, we could see a lot of students heading toward the campus.

I smiled, "I guess. I guess I am..."

"Well, ma'an, let's go..." John loudly requested.

We all jumped into the van and headed quickly across to the campus. Kelly flashed her press identification to the security officer, allowing us to enter the university's grounds.

While heading toward an open area with steps near a building, students began to accumulate in the immediate area.

A student set up a microphone at the bottom where the stage of the quad was located. The quad was designed much like an ancient Greek theater, formed out of a valley with the stage being at the lowest elevation. A student continued to tap the mic and then said, "Testing, Testing." The mic was hooked-up to speakers which surrounded the quad.

John set up the camera facing the steps and then announced, "Go ahead... I'm ready."

Kelly gently held my hand, leading me to the top of the steps. She then began speaking. "Hello! I'm Kelly Babonivitz here with Jerry Fletcher, who was missing last weekend at Red Rock Canyon and, later, mysteriously disappeared. And then, after eight hours passed, he then reappeared. He is here to tell you his experience and the truth about what really happened, and not the fabricated version that was portrayed by Metro. Now, here is Jerry Fletcher!"

Great, loud applause came from the anticipating students. I tapped the mic. THUMP. THUMP. And I then said, "It really works." The crowd immediately broke out into laughter.

When the crowd became quiet again, suddenly, thick, dark thunder-like clouds began to move overhead. A brilliant deep reddish hue of light was emanating from the edges of the thick, dark clouds.

I looked into the crowd, seeing all the mixed faces and then began to say, "I want to thank everyone here for coming here on such short notice."

"Go for it, Jerry!!! Tell it like it is!" a student yelled out.

I smiled; the clouds overhead continued to thicken, and I continued, "Well, where do I begin?"

"From the beginning, Jerry! From the beginning!" the same student shouted.

The crowd laughed and again subsided. I then continued, "Last Saturday, I did not fall, slip, or bump my head. I did not have a concussion. What did happen is something that... Well, you all might think that I'm crazy. Nuts... or a damn fool for even coming up here to speak about it, but it's the truth." I momentarily paused while clearing my throat and then confidently announced, "I was abducted. No I can't say that... I was transported. I was transported to an alien starship that was hovering above Lake Mead."

While only the campus remained mysteriously dry from the torrential onslaught of surrounding rain, the sudden heavy downpour continued to drench the remainder of Las Vegas.

Several dark-suited men and women with earplugs began to surround the perimeter of the crowd while I continued my speech. "The starship was quite majestic... There were crystals everywhere... Gold ones... Blue ones... And green ones and large purple ones... An alien approached me... He was tall with platinum blonde hair... He looked humanlike. Later, I was introduced to the other aliens on the starship, and they all looked like us. All were quite different from each other, being very multi-racial. Some were quite tall and some were short. And there were also children-like aliens with very large heads that I learned latter were quite telekinetic. Well, anyway, this platinum alien held up his palms, opening his finger in a "V" shape and said..." I held my hand up toward the audience with a split-fingered "V."

"What did he say, Jerry?! What did he say?!" a student yelled out from the crowd.

Again, the audience laughed. I saw that the students were quite intensely focused on what I had to say, so I continued to explain away. I elaborated how the aliens were Star souls from the Orion and Pleaidian star systems. Like a professor giving a lecture, I continued to explain the relationship of the aliens' history with our own. While I was elaborating about Star souls and Earth souls, with surprising effect, I saw that the students quickly related to the information while it seemed to pour out from my tongue. I lectured about the how the Light and Dark were in

72

their constant war, and how we were very much part of this integrating battle for Earth. The students confirmed my explanation of the "Dark" corrupting powers within the governments, religious institutions, and the corporations of today. I felt like Martin Luther King at Washington, giving his famous speech, "I have a dream." But this was no dream and no political theory, but a reality of the world around us.

All during my speech, the heavy rain continued to spray down upon Las Vegas, while all the quad area remained dry. Thunder and lightning would alternately rumble throughout the sky.

Above Las Vegas in cloaking state in a different sub-spatial time dimension, two starships were exchanging fire upon each other, utilizing light beams and sub-spatial torpedoes... With each blast, a wave of energy would ripple across the horizon. Atmospheric pressure on Earth would chaotically fluctuate. Both starships continued their dogfight, each trying to destroy the other. Their ships would spin and twirl, disappear and appear, all maneuvering in their special chess game of space war. But suddenly, a heavy light burst discharged from one of the starships. The star light burst ripped into the hull of the other starship. As if being absorbed, the star light burst began to engulf, swallowing the starship whole until there was only a small pin light of what was left of the starship. And then suddenly the pin light quietly disappeared.

Suddenly, back on the Earth plane, in Las Vegas while I continued to explain what was shown to me by the alien, the sky above opened up with a sudden, brilliant appearance of a very large rainbow manifesting itself just above the university. Everyone suddenly was quiet and in awe admiring the brilliant panoramic view of this rainbow manifestation above. The rain had stopped, while the clouds quickly dissipated. A gentle breeze then crossed the campus. The cool spring like breeze refreshed and cleansed the air. Suddenly, I heard a bird chirp. "You all heard the little bird. I guess he wants me to continue." I smiled and the students laughed.

Then I continued with the explanation of my inspiring dogma and the biblical history. I elaborated about the angels and the different souls, and, of course, what we thought were miracles, but were actually causations of aliens. At that very moment, I looked within the audience for that deranged idiot who was going to shoot me like I was John Lennon. But seeing that there was no barrel in the distance pointing toward me, I continued even while the feds and the cops began to tighten their encirclement of the quad.

And so I concluded with, "These institutions used religion to gain power. They used guilt and fear as methods of control. Now, the dark souls have evolved using the monetary system or economic system to control the masses.

Have you noticed how corporations are now in control of the governments worldwide? Quite similar to the religious institutions controlling the governments in the past... The religious institutions, corporations, and governments are married into the same covenant of the DARK. And now, the aliens of the LIGHT have come back in force to counter the DARK on the Earth plane. This war between LIGHT and DARK has been a continual war..."

Suddenly, the feds converged upon the students. From behind the buildings, campus police joined forces with the feds and Metro Police, and while trying to advance toward me and Kelly, they all began to ruthlessly beat any student who stood within their path. The students began to defend themselves.

Additional Metro Police appeared from the street side on Maryland Parkway. The Metro Police started shooting their canisters of tear gas at us and the students. The feds, riot geared Metro Police, and campus police then began to fall back. The students threw the canisters of tear gas back at their attackers. Rubber bullets began whizzing by the students as they ducked for cover.

Metro riot police with their shields held high were protecting themselves from the onslaught of bottles and rocks, and while pointing their guns toward the students marched in unison like the "goose step" of Hitler's army. They continued to discharge their weapons at the students. This was Las Vegas in the year 2006 and not Berkeley of 1969. It was like Kent State all over again.

Through all the commotion and the smoke-filled air, Kelly, John, and I managed to sneak out of the Las Vegas riot. We quickly jumped into our van and headed off.

CHAPTER 12

A RUDE AWAKENING

Martin, meanwhile, was in a meeting with Richard, the manager of the graphic department in his office. The office lights were dimmed to create an intimidating aura. Richard's intention was to utilize any method of intimidation to ultimately get what he wanted.

"Marvin, I want you to continue putting the pressure on everyone. Harass the shit out of them, if need be. There are to be no individuals in this department. Only hard- working drones!"

Marvin asked. "What about Danny and Joe?"

"What about them?"

"They're going to give me problems."

"You answer only to me! And if they have a problem with that, then I will deal with them accordingly. All right?"

"All right." Marvin hesitated and then asked, "What about Fletcher?"

"Deal with him! Put the pressure on him! Find something. He has too much influence with the drones. He's like a cancer in here. Hell, he thinks that it's America in this department. Well, it isn't! And I don't want his fucking individualistic crap spreading in this department. So go find something!"

"I tried before, but he does his work so efficiently."

"Well, go find something or make something up that you can write him up for. I want him in my palm. Understand?" Richard clenched his fist.

Marvin nodded and then quietly left, entering the main facility of warehouse in the graphics department. To his surprise, everyone was gone except for Danny and Joe.

"Where's everyone?" Marvin asked.

Danny replied, "They all headed into the break room. Apparently, Fletcher's on TV..."

"Hey, I don't know about you, but I gotta see this. So, Danny, are you coming?" Joe asked while getting up and heading to the door.

"Of course, Fletcher on TV, I wouldn't miss it." Danny smiled back and then followed Joe out to the break room while poor bewildered Marvin stood watching his co-supervisors leave.

In the break room, everyone was huddled, glued around the television.

Just as Joe and Danny entered, everyone was focused on the television, and the newscaster announced, "Hello! This is Nina Fernandez at Channel Four News with late-breaking news. After an exclusive interview with our correspondent Kelly Babonivitz at UNLV, Jerry Fletcher, earlier this morning, was giving his explanation before a large group of students about his mysterious disappearance at Red Rock Canyon last weekend, when a massive riot broke out between the students and the authorities. But first, here is a live taping of Fletcher's speech just prior to the riot."

Kelly now came into view standing next to me. I then came into focus while speaking. "...Quite similar to the religious institutions controlling the governments in the past. The religious institutions, corporations, and governments are married into the same covenant of the DARK. Now, the aliens of the LIGHT have come back in force to counter the DARK on the Earth plane. This war between LIGHT and DARK has been a continual war..."

Suddenly, the police and suited men and women converged on the students while trying to head toward me.

Students were being clubbed. We heard shots being fired.

Riot police lined up while taking aim and firing upon the students. Students were being pelted by rubber bullets and canisters of tear gas. It resembled the Chicago riots outside the Democratic Convention in 1968.

The news anchor came back into view. "I apologize, but we have late-breaking news from around the world as well as nationally. Riots have suddenly broken out in Los Angeles, San Diego, San Francisco, Portland,

and Seattle on the West Coast. Riots have also broken out in Minneapolis, Cleveland, and in the northeast in New York, Boston, and Newark. The National Guard has been called in by their respective governors. These governors have declared a state of emergency.

"Meanwhile, in Europe and Asia, riots have also broken out. France, Germany, and Britain have declared martial law.

"In Beijing, China, thousands of demonstrators who were protesting for democratic civil liberties were surprisingly joined by some of the Chinese military, who were in dissent of the present government. With this sudden division of power, the Chinese government is desperately trying to prevent a collapse.

"Meanwhile, in the Middle East, Israeli tanks and air support along with the Palestinian and Israeli infantry surprisingly attacked Jordan and seized Amman. The Jordanian army was quickly subdued, and thus the Hashemite King has abdicated his throne. The Palestinians raised their flag in Amman, declaring that Jordan is now Palestine. This was a direct reversal of the 1970 civil war where the Israelis defended the Hashemite Kingdom from the Palestinians. There is speculation that apparently in secrecy, the Israelis and Palestinians formed a covert alliance to their subsequent peace initiative. It was disclosed by both prime ministers that both nations would share joint control of the West Bank and that Rammallah would become the capital of Palestine. The Israelis and Palestinians apparently covertly entered into a mutual defense and economic pact which we now know was called the Covenant of Abraham.

"While the anarchy around the world and here locally is trying to be contained by their respective governments, economic chaos developed when the FBI discovered that a virus called the 'Love Worm' entered the government computer systems, thus paralyzing the IRS and other financial operations performed by the government. The FBI said that they are currently trying to remedy the situation while investigating the culprits. The virus has apparently not entered into any of the government's communication systems."

The news anchor suddenly stopped, while putting her hand on her ear then continued, "Excuse me, but we bring you a live message from the President of the United States, President Halliburton."

Sitting behind his desk in the Oval Office, President Halliburton began, "Good evening. As you may have already been informed, our great nation has been under attack for the last twenty-four hours. Terrorists have initiated riots and lawlessness in our major cities. These terrorists have threatened our way of life. They have waged war on our law-abiding citizens. So to protect our great nation from this anarchy and terrorism, I've declared martial law throughout the United States. I assure you that these evildoers will be contained, apprehended, and then prosecuted. I will, with all my means, maintain order in our great nation. And I wish to thank the American people for their patience and patriotism in these dark times... God bless America. Thank you."

The television was turned off.

Everyone in the room looked at one another. There was mumbling within the room. The exchanging thoughts of what they had just witnessed were rampantly running through the room.

Marvin and Richard entered the break room. "Everyone back to work!" Marvin shouted.

Everyone remained motionless while just glaring at the two. Richard then commanded, "You heard him! Get back to work!"

Suddenly, from somewhere in the crowd, someone shouted back, "Fuck you!"

Richard demanded, "Who said that?!"

Suddenly, Jed stood up and proclaimed, "I did!"

Richard then began to reply, "All right then you're..."

But suddenly Lennon stood up. "No, I did!"

And then Linda and Sherry stood up, "No, we did!"

Then Jethro stood up, and then everyone stood up, shouting in unison, "FUCK YOU!"

Richard began to scream out, "Then you're all..." when suddenly, the group began humming "The Battle Hymn of the Republic" while marching out of the building.

Richard just mumbled while watching in disbelief, "Fired..."

CHAPTER 13

TIME TO BREATHE FRESH AIR

I was reclining on a couch in a cabin in the midst of Mt. Charleston.

Mt. Charleston, with its high forest terrain, overlooked the Las Vegas basin, giving the locals here an alternative to the harsh desert heat during the summer months.

During the violent encounter at UNLV, Kelly, John and I discreetly sneaked out by changing from one car to another. Now that we were in Mt. Charleston, Kelly thought that it would best if we just "hung low" from the authorities while we contemplated our next move.

I didn't know whose cabin this was, but it was really picturesque. The cabin was situated on a secluded foothill, with a thick pine forest at the base and a serene view of the mountain at the rear. There were several bedrooms including a loft on top where Kelly was sound asleep. I guessed that with all the pressure from trying to protect me, which was a twenty-four-hour job unto itself, I would've been exhausted as well.

John was "kicking it" out on a hammock in the back, enjoying the fresh air.

From what I understood, the government had declared that I was a terrorist and that I was responsible for inciting the riots. They had also accused me of kidnapping Kelly.

While leaving Las Vegas, we saw hundreds of jets and helicopters flying out of Nellis Air Force Base. Like a long procession, tanks from the north were heading toward the city. Truckloads of troops in armored personnel carriers followed the tanks. I presumed that they were going to try to maintain order. And of course, we all must be maintained to preserve the status quo of order.

So much had happened in the past few days, I couldn't believe the events that had actually transpired. While at the same time, I felt the paradox of being a participant in an event as well as the surreal observer. It was like the irony of the moment that being the observer and the participant all at the same time, and yet when I stood there lecturing to the students of the past and present; it was so surreal to be a reality and not to reiterate, but it was deja vu.

While in our hiding place, we listened to the news. I was quite overwhelmed by the international outburst of anarchy. But then again, the bubble was about to burst. And like most, I just didn't pay attention to what was really happening in the world around us. But it was a given that the clandestine policy of globalization by the elitists would eventually be challenged in some form or matter, but not like this. This outburst of rebellion was all so sudden and on such an astonishing scale. Was it possible that such events could happen so fast? Was it just a miracle, or a miracle of the "close-encounter kind?" I pondered.

Still, I wasn't surprised by the sudden events in the Middle East. This was just a matter of time. Having lived in Israel for several years, I knew that the people, both Arabs and Israelis, would eventually come to a new alignment as long as outside forces would not be involved. But looking back, when the Palestinians and Israelis had removed all outsiders including the American convoy from the proceedings of negotiations, it was now more obvious that something had been brewing. It seemed that history was turned upside down.

People seemed to quickly forget that present-day Jordan was actually created by the British after World War I per the agreement of "Lawrence of Arabia" and Sheik Abdullah, later King of Trans-Jordan (today called Jordan), Jordan was really the cut-out of the Palestine Mandate, thus in reality was really the Arab Palestine, while Israel was really being the remainder. In other words, the reason the majority of Jordan was Palestinian is quite simply that it was part of the Palestine Mandate.

So while peace between the Israelis and the Palestinians became almost an inevitable event, a joint military attack against Jordan, not even the U.S. or anyone could have imagined it. But then again, the politics of the Middle East is not something that the average Westerner could comprehend. Hell, the people in the region can't even comprehend it. But still its amazing how enemies could be suddenly the best of friends. Perhaps it was just another "miracle."

And then there was China. The people of China had finally risen up against their totalitarian government. Though this has happened many times before, this time, some of the military had actually joined in the protest—an event that was astonishing in its own right. Or perhaps again, it was just another "miracle."

The cataclysmic events of what had just transpired may seem all but surreal, but when they actually do happen, then the so-called experts would have to create their imaginary theories to justify logically why certain political events would or could occur. But when has world politics actually conformed to logic? The world is but a round peg that can't be put into a square hole. Wow, did I just think of that... I guessed that my mind was running on high octane. Well, it has been ever since my "experience."

Well anyway, I heard that President Halliburton had referred to the students of UNLV as anti-American, anti-Christian, and heathens. It was interesting how all along the West Coast, Northeast, and Northern states, riots had broken out. These were the very same states so called blue states that voted against him in the last presidential election. All the Midwestern and Southern states, though, remained quiet. Oh, I forgot to mention that Halliburton has now called the Internet an instrument of Satan and that its users are "hackers of the devil" who were as amoral as the residents of Sodom and Gomorrah and who should be purged out of existence. Amazing and yet not surprising.

I jumped on the second hammock next to John, who was now sound asleep. While taking a breath of the fresh air, I took in the moment of my tranquil surroundings, and within moments, I too was sound asleep.

CHAPTER 14

NEWS, PAST AND PRESENT

"Hello! It's time to be liberated! Live from Liberation Radio, where the truth comes first!" the radio announcer blasted out.

We were listening to the radio while cruising in an Aerostar, a "family minivan," heading on I-15 toward California in the black of night. While I drove, Kelly was sleeping in the back and John was sitting on the passenger side. We decided not to let Kelly drive. Hell, we wanted to get to California in one piece, if you know what I mean.

"Liberation Radio" continued, "The latest report from the City of Sin, Las Vegas, Nevada... Thousands of Metro Police officers have put down their arms while joining in protest for the liberation of America. The National Guard, meanwhile, has united with the armed forces at Nellis Air Force Base, who unilaterally have declared mutiny against the government.

"In our City of Angels, Los Angeles, thousands of demonstrators of all races and ethnicities, in a united front, are continuing their protest just outside the LAPD's downtown central office.

"As the protestors stormed the city and county government offices, under the shadow of night, the District Attorney's Office of Los Angeles county representatives have slipped out of California and are believed to be under the protection of the Mexican government.

"In not so surprising event, Loren Daniels, the great actor/director/producer known for his political attitudes about changing and fixing the government system has announced that Western and Northern States should unite with the Northeastern States in the liberation of the United States.

"Meanwhile, President John T. Halliburton has instructed the Pentagon to mobilize troops for a massive assault on Las Vegas to cleanse what he called the source or spark of evildoers where the Anti-Christ dwelled.

"On the world scene, across Europe, the smoke has begun to clear, leaving Europe in its transformation liberated, while in Vatican City, the protests surrounding the city continue.

"In Thailand, hundreds of drug and slave lords have been captured. The new liberated State of Thailand has declared capital punishment for child prostitution profiteers and sex slave traders. The new Thai government has informed that they are in the process of creating rehabilitation and self-confidence centers for the victims of these crimes.

"In China, in an effort to control the present turmoil of dissenters within their military, the Chinese government has declared that Tibet is now an independent state. Thousands in Tibet celebrate."

"This is really unbelievable." I astonishingly blurted out, "Who would have thought that there would be a second American revolution being born as we speak? For over two hundred years, the American people were slowly being conditioned to be apathetic drones, while allowing the governments and financial barons dictate their lives. Who would have thought that all the government's supposed control was just a façade, when confronted by the united will of the people? The American people... If Jefferson were alive, he would be so proud."

"Yeah, ma'an, he would be..." John replied.

Suddenly, we heard Bob Marley's song, "Get Up, Stand Up."

After the song finished, I asked, "So John... How did you meet Kelly?"

"Well, you see ma'an, we met at NYU. I was studyin' film while Kel was studyin' journalism, and well, we both had the same documentary class, ma'an. And we ended up doin' a documentary film together. Since then, we've been friends while always workin' together, ma'an."

"Are you two...?"

"No ma'an. She's like my little sista. So don't worry a thing, ma'an."

"Ah, worry?"

"Hey bro, I've see how you both look goo-goo eyed at each otha. Hell, ma'an, there's so much sexual tension in the air that even President Clinton would've blushed."

"Yeah, I kind of..."

"Like her, ma'an..."

"Yeah."

"It's cool, ma'an."

"So what's her story? I mean, why's she so..."

"Schizoid, ma'an."

"Yeah."

"Ma'an, she's been like that all them years I've known her. Her whole life was her grandma-ma."

"Her grandma?"

"Her parents passed away when she was justa young, and apparently she was raised by her grandma-ma. Though a funny thing, she neva mentions anything about them. Ma'an, I guess it's neva been something that she eva wanted to discuss. And..."

"And?"

"I think the rest you'd have to ask yourself..." John stopped and then continued in a very serious tone, "And ma'an, like I said, she's like my little sista... So don't eva fuck with her heart... Especially now she's justa gettin' ova her grandma-ma's death... So don't you be fuckin' with her. You hear, ma'an!"

I stuttered, "Ah, I... I won't... I really..."

John suddenly busted out laughing. "Ma'an, I's justa fuckin' with ya." And then he said, "Hell, ma'an, she might even chew you up and spit you away all the same if you know what I mean, ma'an."

"She might at that," I smiled then asked, "So what about you?"

"About me?"

"Yeah."

"No ma'an, I'm straight."

"No I mean..."

"I know what you mean, ma'an. I was justa fuckin' with ya."

John looked down and there was a suddenly awkwardness in the air. It seemed that John would use sarcasm and humor to cover what was really hurting him deep inside. You could almost see it in his eyes.

He suddenly broke the silence. "My love was murdered."

"I'm sorry..."

"Yeah, thanks, ma'an."

"So how was she...?"

"After being pulled ova by a cop, Jasmine was asked to get out of her car, because she fit their profile of someone they were lookin' fo'. She was black, so, ma'an, I guess that fit their fuckin' profile. Well anyway, while she was puttin' her hands behind her head, that's when the cop, ma'an, unloaded on her. That's when he fuckin' killed her."

"I'm... I'm sorry."

"Thanks."

"What happened to the cop?"

"Nothin' as usual, ma'an... In Vegas, if a Metro cop kills, it's considered justified homicide. Neva in the history of Las Vegas, ma'an, has any cop been found convicted of an unjustified murder."

"But still?"

"Like I said, ma'an... In Vegas, a Metro cop is licensed to kill, especially when the victim's a minority... It's all fuckin' bullshit, ma'an... It justa eats me up just thinkin' about it, and it's already been seven months since her death, ma'an. God, I miss her." John looked down, opened his wallet, and gazed at the picture of Jasmine. Though his eyes watered, John tried to discreetly rub his eyes to cover his tearing emotion.

I sympathetically replied, "Hey, man... It's okay. It's okay to cry."

While wiping his face and still gazing upon Jasmine's picture, John hesitantly answered, "But, ma'an, it still fuckin' hurts. I miss her so much. I love her. I will always love her." A tear rolled down his cheek, and splashed upon Jasmine's cheek.

CHAPTER 15

THE TALL STRANGER, A NEW ENCOUNTER

Barstow, California...

Besides Bakersfield, Barstow was the number two trucker's stop of California. Yeah, there was Fresno. And there was Modesto, but everyone stopped in Barstow while heading to and from Las Vegas and Los Angeles.

Up ahead was a bright neon light, "Roy's Truck Stop." We then pulled off the highway and into the large truck stop.

Roy's was something of an enormity. Besides the rows and rows of gas stations, the inside had long, winding stores which included restaurants, resting areas, laundry facilities, a television room and entertainment area with video games, pool tables, foosball tables, and boot shine area and, of course, there was the convenience store which, you name it, they've got it. As we entered the store, we noticed that a large group of people had gathered around a television.

On the television, a news anchorman announced, "And on the latest, President Halliburton has declared martial law as the rioting and looting continued in the major metropolitan cities along the East and West Coast. Meanwhile, the FBI has put an all points bulletin for Jerry Fletcher. Fletcher has also been placed on the FBI's Most Wanted List. He was last seen with Kelly Babonivitz, a news reporter for a television station in Las Vegas, who he had abducted shortly after he incited the riots in Las Vegas. Fletcher has an accomplice, a tall black man in his mid-twenties with long braids. If you see him or have knowledge of their whereabouts, please contact the FBI at the phone number shown above. Fletcher is believed to be armed and dangerous."

Kelly asked, "Are you hungry? Do you want something to eat?"

I looked at the counter, and was amazed at the assortment of jerky meats. "Ya got yer beef jerky, rattler meat jerky or rattlesnake jerky, and, of course, then there's yer gator jerky. Sound plum there delicious. Don't it?"

"Ah. Kelly just get me some of them sunflower seeds. I'm going back to the car," I replied.

While exiting the store, I became aware of several people in the store oddly gawking at me.

Moments later, John came out of the store while I was now reclining on the passenger side of the minivan.

In the store, Kelly was busy putting all the snack food on the counter.

"Will that be all for ya?" the thin woman with crooked teeth who was standing behind the counter asked.

"Yeah," Kelly replied.

Suddenly, Kelly was startled by a tap on her shoulder. She turned around, and there was a tall man with shoulder-length blonde hair and deep-set blue eyes curiously smiling at her.

"Sorry to bother you, ma'am... By chance, are you heading toward Los Angeles?" the tall man humbly asked.

"Ah, why yes. Yeah, why?"

"Well, I was on my way from Las Vegas, and my automobile... I mean my car broke down, and I was hoping that you could give me a lift. I'll certainly pay for your gas. And I promise that I won't be much of a bother."

While gazing into the man's eyes, Kelly became mesmerized, "I... I don't think that'll be a problem. We do have plenty of room."

Again in a humble manner, the tall man replied, "Thank you. I really appreciate it. Do you need help with the..."

"No thanks, I got it. So tell me. Where did you say you were coming from?"

"Aahh, Las Vegas."

"Crazy what's bloody happening there," Kelly blurted as they both walked toward the minivan.

"No. Not really."

"Huh?" Kelly suddenly stopped.

And with a smile, the tall man replied, "Destiny... It was destined to happen. Destiny was just manifesting itself on planet Earth. I mean around the world, and here in the United States."

"Wow. You sound like Jerry. You must've been at the rally at UNLV."

"No, but I was near. Quite near. And I did hear everything."

"Oh?" Kelly replied, puzzled, and then pointed. "Our van's over yonder."

"Who's that coming with Kelly?" I nudged John.

John sat up and looked. "Ma'an, got me." John then rolled down his window and yelled. "Kel, we gotta get goin', ma'an!"

"I know. I know. I know," Kelly replied after reaching the minivan, and turned toward the tall man. "Also... Excuse me, but I've seem to have forgotten your name."

The tall man returned, "I'm Yo'shu... I'm Joshua."

"Umm, Joshua needs a ride to L.A."

Joshua handed over a hundred-dollar bill. "For your gas."

"Hundred bucks for gas! Ma'an, we're headin' to L.A., not Hawaii." John shook his head.

"Then take it for the inconvenience."

"Ma'an, now like why would there be any inconvenience? Are you anticipatin' some kinda problem?" John returned.

"John, he's just trying to be considerate." Kelly lashed out.

"Justa tryin' to be extra cautious that's all, Kel. Gotta to be extra careful, if you know what I mean." John winked.

"Right." Kelly nodded.

"Hop in the back. Make ya self at home, ma'an," John commanded.

I looked back at our new passenger; light shined on the stranger's face, giving me a clearer view of his features. He looked so familiar. The stranger smiled. "How are you?"

"Fine. Fine. But you certainly look familiar."

"All strangers can look familiar."

"What?" I replied.

"Maybe we met in a prior lifetime. Or a prior time." Joshua smiled as John started the minivan.

"Yeah, perhaps another time." While shaking my head, I began to wonder, "Where the hell did I see him before?" But I was drawing a blank. It was like when you know something but you can't place your finger on it. Well, that's how I felt. So who was he? But since no one including Kelly seemed all that concerned, I thought that he was all right. He certainly didn't look like a serial killer. I looked at him again, but he had this funny smirk like he knew what was up, and we had to find out the secret on our own.

We turned onto the on-ramp and began heading back on our journey on the I-15 toward Los Angeles.

CHAPTER 16

SHORT TRIP, LONG CONVERSATION

While still "a" cruising along the "Eye" Fifteen, we were listening to the jammin' radio. "Well, well, well! Hope you like the 'Rage?!' And if you didn't, too effing bad! Because this is Liberation Radio! Where the news is truth! And the Rage is on!

"And on the liberation scene, Minnesota Governor Johnny Lofton has declared an alliance with Ohio, New York, Pennsylvania, Massachusetts, Oregon, Washington, and California in our struggle to liberate America. Meanwhile, Loren Daniels from California acknowledged the alliance. Maine and New Hampshire have declared neutrality. Come on guys, it's time get off the fence and join in the fight.

"Meanwhile, news is... Government troops are mobilizing to the bordering states in the north and in Nevada. Come on, Mr. President, bring it on. We're waiting for your ass!

"Well, President Halliburton has called the secession of these States a slap in the face of the Union. Sorry, Mr. President. The only slap in the face has been on the American people.

"The people have risen, Mr. President. You have not been a government for the people, by the people, or of the people. For over two hundred years, the Jeffersonian democracy has been dissolved, crushed, and stamped out, so that a corporate Hamiltonian lordship with an illusionary democratic government could persist in Washington D.C. No more like a plutocracy here, Mr. President!

"Sorry, Mr. President, but the American people have said enough is enough!

"Meanwhile, news of defecting government troops has caused great concern to the D.C. government. Halliburton has announced that any soldier caught defecting will be tried as a treasonable offense, with the death penalty as its sentence.

"Well, I'm feelin' a little beastie now, so here are some more Beastie Boys. 'So What'cha Want.' Oh yeah!"

Beastie Boys music came on, and everyone in the van began semi-dancing to the tunes while I was now driving and John was tokin' a hit of his smoke.

John tried to hold it in while inhaling, but then he wheezed out a small cough as he exhaled, "Hey ma'an, you want some?"

"No man, I'm fucking driving," I answered.

"Kel?" John held out the joint.

Then to everyone's surprise, Joshua replied while taking the joint, "Don't mind if I do..." And then he deeply sucked on the joint in a continuous inhale. In one inhale, he smoked nearly the entire joint. Everyone just stared in shock as he handed back the joint. "Not bad. Not bad at all. Though, I've never tasted such an unusual brand of tobacco."

Kelly then explained, "Ah, Joshua. That was a joint."

"A 'joint?'"

John added, "Yeah, a fuckin' joint, ma'an. You know, ganja..."

"Oh yeah, right. I know. Marijuana," Joshua then pompously returned. "Did I say tobacco? I meant marijuana. Well, haven't tasted such a brand since the days of Colombian gold and Panama red."

John then laughed, "Ma'an, you're an old hippie. I wouldn't of neva guessed."

Joshua bantered while holding his fingers in the peace sign, "Peace, love, sex, and rock and roll! Those were the days!"

"Ma'an, I'll take a hit on that any day..." And John sucked up the remainder of his joint and coughed out as he exhaled the pungent smoke.

"So Joshua, why are you bloody heading to L.A. anyway?" Kelly inquired.

"A business trip... I have a very important business meeting there."

So Kelly continued her Q & A. "So what happened to your car?"

"My water pump went out. I mean it blew up," Joshua quickly answered.

"Huh?"

"I mean my radiator hose blew up, and my car overheated."

I replied, "I know that feeling. That could really fuck up your day."

"So why are you all heading to L.A.?" Joshua asked.

"Road trip," Kelly answered.

"Yeap. Road trip," I blurted out.

"Oh, road trip?" Joshua then kindly asked. "Well if you don't know anyone in L.A., maybe I could help."

"Why do you ask?" I asked.

"Well, I thought perhaps if you had no place to stay or didn't know anybody, I supposed that... Well, actually, I'm supposed to contact someone in Los Angeles during my business trip and..."

"Who?" Kelly quickly asked.

"Well, Loren Daniels. Do you know a Loren Daniels?"

"The director?" Kelly responded.

"The producer," John interjected.

"But he was a great fuckin' actor, too," I added.

"He was a fuckin' great actor, ma'an," John concurred.

"He is. Not was. He's still alive. And he's leading the American revolt in California," Kelly lectured.

Everyone was suddenly awkwardly quiet.

After several moments, Kelly asked, breaking the sudden awkward silence, "So what do you bloody do in Las Vegas?"

"Do?"

"Do? Like what do you do professionally in Vegas?"

"Well, I'm a businessman."

"I figured that... But what kind of business?"

"Astrophysics."

"Astro what, ma'an?" John asked, still high from the pot.

Just as Joshua was about to answer, while we were entering the El Cajon Pass, two Apache helicopters hovered in front of us with their intense lights blinding us. We stopped when out of nowhere, two Abram tanks pulled ahead, aiming their long turrets in our direction. Additional tanks maneuvered themselves, creating a barricade, preventing us from crossing. But we weren't planning to go anywhere.

"What the bloody hell is going on?!" Kelly hysterically shouted.

The two helicopters continued to hover above with their bright lights keeping us in sight. Three armored personnel carriers pulled up and suddenly soldiers leaped out with their automatic weapons pointed.

A jeep suddenly pulled up, and a soldier on a loudspeaker commanded, "This is a secured area! Do not move!"

A group of armed militia quickly and methodically approached us.

One of the militia commanded, "Put your hands on heads and slowly exit the vehicle!"

As we followed his instructions, a helicopter lowered down, landing itself adjacent the jeep. With their weapons still pointing at us, we stood alongside the jeep while being frisked, then handcuffed and blindfolded.

The same militia commanded, "All right! Take them in the copter!"

We were then escorted to the helicopter. While we were being airlifted, I wondered what the fuck was happening. Were we going to be tortured now that we've been caught? Many indiscriminate thoughts of the worst came into my mind, but still I tried to show that I was calm and collected.

While listening to the whirling of the propellers as we took flight, I kept my composure with the hope that something good would actually come of this, but what exactly? What awaited us?

CHAPTER 17

WELCOME TO HOLLYWOOD...

Still blindfolded and bound, we were quickly escorted into a very large, musty room and then pushed into some chairs.

And then we were explained (if you could call it that) that it would be best for us to remain quiet. In other words, "Shut the fuck up!"

We still had no idea where we were, or who our captors were, but we could only assume.

It was very quiet almost to the point that I could hear my heart beat, but it was the clock overhead that I was hearing. Suddenly, there was a murmur in the room. Then a door opened and closed. Though there was an awkward stillness, I heard people mumbling in the background.

Suddenly, the door opened and closed again, and then I could sense that there was again an awkward stillness by those in the room. A man bellowed out in a commanding voice, "Why the hell are they blindfolded and handcuffed! Remove them now!"

My blindfold was quickly removed, and the glaring fluorescent light came into view. But as my blurring vision adjusted to the lighting in the room, I could see that we were seated at a very long, dark oak conference table with rows of leather-upholstered oak chairs.

"Good. I apologize for any inconvenience and abuse that you all were subjected through in order to get you all here," the man sympathetically expressed.

As my eyes continued to adjust themselves to the bright lights, I saw Loren Daniels seated at the head of the table with our tall stranger friend, Joshua, who was standing just behind him, while at Daniels' side were suited men and women, along with uniformed military, the elite officer type—generals, colonels, etc.

Daniels continued, "Again I'm sorry. They were ordered to immediately detain you and then bring you here safe and sound. You apparently were discovered in Barstow, and we could not take the chance that the government forces might apprehend you. If you were caught by them, well... Well, thank God you weren't that's all."

We all looked at each other in awe.

"Oh, by the way, I'm Loren Daniels. And you are in the Central Command of California headquarters for the Liberation of the United States. Hopefully, you all are aware of the civil war which has erupted, since your catalytic speech at UNLV yesterday."

Kelly replied. "Yes, we're all quite aware. But why are we here?"

"For your safety... Oh by the way, Jerry... May I call you Jerry?"

"Ah, yes."

"Your daughter's safe and sound at Miramar. And might I say that she's a bit of a pistol. I guess she gets it from her old man." Daniels chuckled and then continued, "She'll be sent north shortly to join you."

"Why? Or rather how did you come to her whereabouts and why am I here?"

"To answer your question, from some of our sources... We have many operatives in the government from various agencies who have also joined in our effort."

"Spooks?"

"Some call them that. But the important thing is that you're all here safe and sound." He sighed and explained, "Well, presently Halliburton is preparing an invasion against Nevada and Pennsylvania. There is a strategic reason for this, as well as political one. Here." Daniel motioned to an officer. The officer laid down a clear map with orange and blue crayon-like doodling. Daniels continued, "We have obtained a large military force. Most of the armed services are allied with respect to their state affiliation. But others have recently defected from the government to support the revolt as well. We have air support in Miramar, Edwards, and along with our bases up along the West Coast. And of course, we maintain control of Nellis. That is why Halliburton wants to strike Nevada first. And he also wants to split the coalition by knifing through Pennsylvania."

"The coalition?" John asked.

"I'm sorry. Let me bring you up to date, since so much has happened. You see... Washington, Oregon, and California are allied in the revolt. We also just formed an alliance with the Eastern and Northern States. The Midwestern States and Southern States have either announced their neutrality or aligned themselves with Halliburton. While Canada has backed us, Mexico has formally notified that they are allied with the government forces, but they're of no real concern. Mexico's up in a pile of shit of their own with Costa Rican and Nicaraguan forces supporting the Indian revolt in the Yucatan. The rebels have just recently broken through the Mexican front and are presently moving north toward Mexico City."

"I don't know, but it seems that world has gone fucking berserk," I blurted out.

"Yes and no. Things were brewing for some time now, Jerry. It's just that your speech seemed to pop the bubble, igniting the world to wake up and finally take a stand."

"Oh come on now!" I said.

"Not just your speech itself, but the timing of your speech is what literally ignited the massive revolt that would change and liberate the world. I know it's hard to believe, but today in the era of fast information and the Internet, your speech went quickly around the world. It's like you heard of how 'the shot that was heard around the world' in the American Revolution. In this case, it was how your speech was heard around the world. And by the way, that's why Halliburton would love to see your head on the end of a pole."

"You mentioned Canada. What about Canada?" Kelly asked.

"The Canadians are supporting our revolt. In fact, they have sent a mechanized division along with artillery and tanks into Minnesota to back the North."

"Didn't know that Canada had much of an army," I replied.

"Not much, but they are highly trained and highly technical." Daniels then pointed to the north. "Now, Lofton in Minnesota has united the Northern States while Jackson in New York has united the Northeastern States."

I interjected, "Now come on! How the hell are we going to defend ourselves against the massive power that the government forces have? They've got satellites, cruise missiles, and nukes. Well?"

Daniels answered, "The satellites are incapacitated for some unknown reason. Neither they nor we have access to them. Now regarding missiles, we certainly have our share of those. And I don't think even Halliburton is that dumb to use any nukes. But Jerry, we have a very serious and capable land and air force. You might say we're quite equally divided, but they have the strategic advantage: that being our forces are split north, east, and west. And that's why his movements were so obvious."

"What about the naval forces?" Kelly asked.

"The navy has declared neutrality." Daniels pointed to the Plexiglas wall that was lit up with a very large map of the United States and continued, "Here you see. This is where they have mobilized. All along the Rockies, they are spearheading a massive invasion in southern Nevada and in Pennsylvania in the northeast. So our main counterattack will come from two areas. With our marines and paramilitary, we must hold out in Nevada at all cost while protecting Nellis from the initial onslaught. All the while with the 107 Airborne, our Rangers and the Canadians, we will be striking NORAD at their rear. Our problem is time. Nellis must hold out long enough for us to overwhelm NORAD, allowing us to then cut off the rear of their attacking force against Las Vegas, and thus isolating their initial striking divisions from any support."

"Wow, quite bloody impressive! But how did you get all this intelligence?" Kelly asked

"Like I said, we do have our operatives still in D.C. who are giving us very reliable info."

"Like Joshua?" John blurted out.

"Who?" Daniels returned.

"Joshua," Kelly said.

"Joshua! Your operative, Joshua..." I replied.

We all looked up, and there was no sign of Joshua. In bewilderment, John, Kelly, and I just looked at each other.

97

"Ma'an, he was right there. Kel, you saw him," John mumbled.

"Yeah, I know," Kelly mumbled back.

"Jerry, here look. Tell me what you think," Daniels replied while gesturing toward the map.

While scanning the large wall map, I mumbled, "The West... the East... hmmmm... You said that the navy was neutral."

"So, Jerry, what are you thinking?"

"Well, I don't know about your 'Alamo' hold out in Las Vegas, but I would think that the least likely place that Halliburton would expect an attack, because it would certainly be an obvious one..." I pointed my finger on the map on Washington D.C. while smiling. "The White House... A clandestine attack on the White House... This alone might create enough of a diversion. I don't think it will help your time problem with saving Nellis, but it would certainly give Halliburton a good run for his money."

Kelly blurted out, "Jerry, are you fucking bloody crazy? No one in their right mind would think that they could attack the White House! Do you know how secure the White House is?!"

"Exactly, the White House... Now that would be a surprise," Daniels replied in agreement.

"Huh?" Kelly uttered.

Daniels continued, "Halliburton would never expect an all-out attack on the White House. It would be his most vulnerable area. His Achilles' heel..."

"What about the feds? You know, the FBI, CIA etc.?" Kelly asked.

Daniels chuckled, "Those morons. The FBI is still fucking around with who sabotaged their computers, and the CIA is all but inept. I don't even think that the Mossad could even save their ass this time that is if they really would. Hell, they're all scrambling around with the NSA and the IRS trying save their fucking money. And thanks to 'Hackers Unite,' all of their computers are so full of viruses that even the best penicillin couldn't fix them. Again all thanks to 'Hackers Unite.' Oh, by the way, they're the very ones who transmitted your speech all over the world via the Internet. Imagine the nerds and the geeks of the world are the revolutionary heroes of today. So anyway, like I said, the feds don't know their heads from their asses."

"But ma'an, what about the NSA and the CIA?" John asked, still feeling his high from his smoke during the drive.

Daniels looked at John, perplexed. I thought, "Hell, does he have to repeat the whole damn thing again?" So I sarcastically smirked. "Too much Cheech and Chong on the way here, if you know what I mean..."

Daniels shook his head while laughing and patting John on the back. "Well, after this whole damn thing is over, you and I are goin' to have do some serious partying, but for right now, we all must stay focused."

Daniels walked across to the map and continued, "John, their finances were sort of tied up and the Treasury Department has no real money. Their electronic funds are now all gone or tied up, if you know what I mean. So without funds, and with a fucked-up computer system, all the government agencies have been neutered. And again, all thanks to 'Hackers Unite.' So like I said, the government agencies are no real threat."

"That's why Halliburton called the hackers, the evil doers of the anti-Christ?" I said.

Daniels smiled. "Yeap. Well, anyway, Jerry, your idea of a massive attack on the White House does have merit. But how could we create such a massive attack without being discovered?"

I returned, "You said that Halliburton plans to have a large-scale attack in Nevada and Pennsylvania. Well, hell, he'll be creating our own diversion. When he attacks, that's when we have to attack the White House."

"Yes. Yes, I see what you mean." And with a smile, Daniels turned toward me, looking straight into my eyes. "Jerry, where did you come up with this stuff?"

"I watch a lot of movies. And I've seen all yours," I smiled back.

With a smile, Daniels asked, "All of them?"

"Yeah, all of them."

Daniels, still with his gleaming smile, replied, "Well, maybe, Hollywood does have a positive influence after all."

"Amen to Hollywood." I praised with somewhat of a gloat.

"Well, in the meantime, I'll have to contact Lofton and Jackson and get their input on your strategy. But for right now, I don't know about you, but I'm really hungry."

Suddenly, we heard John's stomach growl, and everyone broke out laughing.

John smiled now that he was just coming down from his high.

"I guess that means yes," Daniels concluded. Everyone broke into another volley of laughter.

CHAPTER 18

SEX, TRUTH AND THE EQUATION OF SPIRITUAL TIME

After an interesting meal, and having experienced a long and perhaps extraordinary day, we all retired to our quarters.

While lying on a bed in my quarters, I pondered, "So much... And yet so fast... Events, they sometimes move with their own idiosyncrasy of time. Some say that when you get old, the days and weeks become years. If that is so, then I must be a thousand years old today. But are these global events moving like Superman with the speed of light or are they just the eminent revolution of mankind?"

Since my experience, my mind had become ever more focused while my senses had also expanded to new levels. My smell, sight, hearing, and touch all became extraordinarily sensitive.

I closed my eyes and then Kelly's face became illustrated within my mind. For the moment, the pressure of the ongoing political events subsided. I thought of Kelly's lips on mine. She had such a sweet smell about her, like she was naturally perfumed. Ah, maybe I was just being too sensitive, but I was truly feeling emotionally attached to her. But then it's been such a short time. But then again it wasn't long ago that I was just another schnook doing the nine-to-five thing. And it was only last Saturday that I had my encounter. But still... Love has no timing. It is only eventful. It just happens when it happens. I guess that's what has made love such a mystery. It simply has a mind of its own. Damn, I was feeling a distinct euphoria, when suddenly there was hard rapping at my chamber door and not the Edgar Allan Poe kind.

I shouted, "The door's open! Come in!" But the knocking continued. So I finally got my lazy ass up and walked up to the door. Ooops... It was locked.

After I finally opened the damn door, Kelly pushed her way into my room and lashed out, "Thanks for finally opening the bloody door!"

I stuttered, "Well... I..."

Kelly mimicked back, "I... I... I what... What... What... The door was fucking bloody locked!"

"What's your problem?!"

"What do think? You're my fuckin' problem!"

"I'm your problem?"

"Yeah, you're my problem, and I need to answer the equation to my bloody problem," Kelly sarcastically replied and then shoved me with her hands. Catching me off guard, I toppled onto my bed.

Kelly immediately climbed on top of me. With a passionate glaze upon her face, she restrained my arms with her legs.

Kelly then smiled, "Don't you think it's time to quit child math and we move on to calculus?" And with that she leaned over and placed her lips on mine. Kelly and I passionately kissed. All the while, I responded to each of her sensual attacks with an equally sensual response.

Our bodies mashed into a continuity of carnal erotic movements. Our bodies gyrated in an ecstatic rhythm as we continued our lip dance.

Kelly began licking my lips with her flickering tongue, targeting my neck with her erotic attack. Suddenly, I moaned as her teeth, like "Bram's Dracula," sunk into my flesh. Her suckling on my neck continued while moaning in unison as small drippings of my crimson blood surfaced from her feeding.

Kelly suddenly sat up, wiping her mouth. A wild glaze emerged from her face, and then she immediately tore open my shirt, exposing my chest and stomach. Kelly frantically began kissing, licking, and biting my chest and stomach. While she continued caressing her lips and tongue against my exposed skin, she softly caressed my genitals. You know my "cock and balls." I became aching hard. She opened my pants, exposing me to her awaiting mouth. As she took me into her hot succulent mouth, I moaned.

I opened her blouse and bra exposing her gentle, perking breasts. As she brushed her erect nipples along my exposed skin, she moaned. Kelly then placed my manhood between her breasts while pleasuring me with her flute playing tongue. I tried to open her pants, but she brushed my hands away. As she continued to please me, I tried again to open her pants.

"Baby... I want to please you as well," I softly whispered while kissing her neck.

"Not now... Another time for that, but not today... Baby, I want you to cum... To cum in my mouth," Kelly replied and then continued her suckle while pumping my rod into her mouth.

I moaned.

"Come on, baby. Shoot your love into my mouth. I want to taste your love in my mouth," Kelly sensually whispered.

She continued pleasing me with her licking of my scrotum while stroking me up and down. Kelly now placed me within her lips while rubbing my mushroom helmet against her the roof of her mouth. She began to moan like there was some kind of "g" spot in the roof of her mouth. Her sudden excitement lit me up to the point that I suddenly lost control and exploded myself into her awaiting mouth. Kelly suddenly yelled out like a wild animal moaning into an unimaginable climax. As her body convulsed and twitched, Kelly continued to heavily drain me of my fluids. I felt so disoriented. The room seemed to be spinning. Around and around it went... I felt her energy mixing with mine. As she withdrew my last drop, emptying myself completely, our bodies spastically convulsed. I felt my spirit, my soul entering hers. We became so lethargic while our bodies intertwined. Kelly collapsed upon me. And then with what little energy she had, she kissed my lips and then placed her head on my chest, closing her eyes with an expression of total satisfaction.

My eyes closed, feeling a very deep bliss.

Our souls continued to be intertwined entering a deep, tantric bliss...

CHAPTER 19

A GETTYSBURG IN THE NEW MILLENNIUM

Ezekiel 32:03

"Thus said the Lord G-D:

I will cast My net over you. In an assembly of many peoples; And you shall be hauled up in My toils. And I will fling you to the ground; Hurl you upon the open field. I will cause all the birds of the sky; To settle upon you. I will cause the beasts of all the earth; To batten on you. I will cast your carcass upon the hills; And fill the valleys with your rotting flesh. I drench the earth; With your oozing blood upon the hills, And watercourses shall be filled with your (gore). When you are snuffed out, I will cover the sky; And darken its stars; I will cover the sun with clouds; And the moon shall not give its light. All the lights that shine in the sky, I will darken above you;   And I will bring darkness upon your land."

At 3:00 A.M., along the Potomac River, the fogging mist covered a squadron of men and woman in black wetsuits who were riding submerged watercraft heading toward the White House.

At 5:55 A.M., in Washington D.C, in the White House, President Halliburton was sitting at a long table in a sub-basement with the remainder of his Joint Chiefs of Staff, along with his security advisors. He stood up and announced, "Initiate Operation Crusade!"

The defense secretary nodded.

A general of the Joint Chiefs picked up the phone and then spoke. While nodding at the defense secretary and Halliburton, the general proclaimed, "We're on."

Halliburton replied with a smirk, "Now, we'll get those motherfuckers once and for all!"

But then suddenly, a series of rockets blasted into the White House. The lights went out, and then suddenly the emergency lights came on. As dust began settling down within the air, Halliburton and his staff huddled underneath the table while the room continued to rumble with each rocket attack.

Like chickens without heads, the marines and Secret Servicemen ran chaotically around the White House as gunfire sprayed toward them. The government's men tried to defend themselves, but the waves of gunfire and rockets continued to overwhelm them.

Hundreds of marines fell to their deaths. Their bodies bled from the piercing rain of gunfire. Body parts and debris flew into the air as rockets exploded.

The center of the White House suddenly collapsed from the second wave of exploding rockets. The ceiling in the sub-basement suddenly buckled, falling onto the table where Halliburton and his associates were huddled. From behind the fallen debris, a marine grabbed Halliburton's hand. "Sir... Mr... Mr. President, come follow us. We must evacuate the White House."

Without hesitation, Halliburton followed the Marine along with his Secret Servicemen out into a lower tunnel leading them out of the White House to an awaiting jet helicopter on the surface lawn.

As Halliburton entered the helicopter, a rocket was launched. And just as the helicopter lifted, the rocket slammed into the ground exploding dirt up into the air, but Halliburton's helicopter miraculously escaped into the smoking sky. His helicopter then disappeared into the southern horizon.

Moments later, the remaining marines and Secret Servicemen in the White House marched out in total humiliation with their hands on top of their heads. The White House forces had surrendered.

The smoldering White House was split into two with the collapsed roof of the center at ground level.

Suddenly, a group of rebel militia climbed up onto one of the split structures and began hoisting two flags. One, the American flag with the word "Liberation" printed in white across the center and the other, the New Jersey state flag. Hundreds cheered to the sight of the two flags being hoisted into the air.

Four black-fatigued rebel militia, two men and two women while hoisting the flags, shouted, "To America! To America! Land of the free! We are America! Land of the free! To the American people, Washington has been liberated!"

At 6:00 A.M. in Los Angeles, the morning was typically overcast for this time of year. Suddenly, from the eastern horizon, a group of low-flying Tomahawk cruise missiles were streaming toward the City of Angels.

Like a whistling wind, they streamed until one exploded and a plume of smoke emerged like the Tower of Babel within Los Angeles while the others splashed into the Pacific.

A cruise missile had just slammed into the Griffith Park Observatory. Kelly and I jolted up from the sudden explosion above. The ground had trembled as the fire alarms suddenly went off.

"It must be an earthquake." I mumbled, still half-asleep.

There was a sudden hard knock at the door. After we quickly threw on our clothes, I opened the door, and a soldier entered, announcing, "You are to come with me! We are under attack."

We followed four soldiers down a long corridor to an awaiting committee of officers and civilians in the "War Room," which contained rows of computers, monitors, and maps. Suddenly, Daniels entered.

A tall mulatto officer with deep piercing blue eyes stood up and explained, "This morning, the government forces launched a series of cruise missiles at Los Angeles. All but one was diverted from their apparent targets and exploded in the Pacific. One did manage to hit the observatory in Griffith Park. At 0600, the government has launched their attack in Las Vegas and Pennsylvania."

Daniels interjected, "Notify all our forces in Nevada to maintain their positions while we initiate our counter-offensive strike."

Another officer in his fifties asked, "Sir, what about the northern forces?"

Daniels answered, "The united northern and eastern fronts will hold their positions. The Canadians, along with our Ranger and Airborne, will discreetly move south into Colorado. I want maximum air support for them." Daniels pointed to a map of the United States and continued, "Last night, I discussed Fletcher's plan of a surprise attack on the White House with Jackson and Lofton, and we all agreed that we had to initiate Operation Jerseymaid. The operation was in progress at 0200 eastern. At 0600 eastern, the 'Jersey Homeboys' attacked the White House. At 0700, I am happy to inform you that we have seized control of the White House. I apologize for not informing you all about the operation. But Lofton, Jackson, and I felt that for this preemptive strike to be successful, we had to limit knowledge of its existence. I hope you all understand that this was not a question of trust. I trust you all. It was determined that if we limit our communications in mentioning this operation, we would limit the chances of government surveillance picking up any knowledge of this operation. Again, I hope you understand."

In unison, everyone responded, "Yes."

"Good," Daniels replied.

Kelly interjected, "What about Halliburton?"

Daniels answered, "He escaped. We believe that he escaped to Texas. The Southern States have continued to declare their loyalty with Halliburton's government."

"Like, ma'an, what about the Midwest?" John then asked.

"They're still aligned with Halliburton, but Montana and Wyoming are now in Canadian control, as both our forces are preparing our move into Colorado."

"Perhaps Halliburton will underestimate the Canadian firepower," I blurted.

"That's what we're hoping," Daniels smiled.

At 6:00 A.M. in Las Vegas, an onslaught of hundreds of F-16s and F-15s swirled down toward Las Vegas Boulevard, "The Strip."

The F-16s launched their air-to-ground missiles. These missiles quickly veered toward their targets. One of the missiles struck within the pyramid structure of the Luxor Hotel, exploding black glass fragments in every direction like an internal volcano.

Two missiles streamed toward the MGM Grand Hotel. Suddenly, one erupted into the base of the front structure of the MGM Grand. The shockwave of this missile's explosion reverberated throughout the streets. Hundreds of people were running for their lives as the second missile slammed into the Golden Lion, the symbol of MGM. The Golden Lion immediately disintegrated into thin air.

All along The Strip, every hotel was today's target practice as the missile onslaught continued. The hotel structures were collapsing faster than the Twin Towers of New York.

Then came the swirling and yet deafening sound of artillery accompanying the sound of the exploding rockets. The sound of destruction, the sound of death is a sound like no other.

Artillery shells and rockets began to strike randomly across eastern Las Vegas. Hundreds of civilians were trying to take cover.

The mixture of human body parts and building debris were flying into the air. There was no screaming of death, but the quiet of lifelessness. War is not hell. War is simply the numbing existence in the state of perpetual purgatory. All life stops.

From Nellis Air Force Base, the rebel forces began their counter-offensive with artillery and rockets of their own while the rebel F-15 fighter jets flew in sweeping from the southwestern horizon. And the dogfight of who will be master of the sky began.

Rebel tanks and ground forces took to their positions in northern Las Vegas. From the north, the rebels began launching artillery toward the encroaching ground forces of the government.

Las Vegas was being turned into a Beirut. The city was evolving into nothing more than a landscape of rubble and cadavers.

Hundreds of people began trying to flee toward the west.

From the east, government tanks with their personnel carriers for support began moving along Boulder Highway heading toward Sahara. Suddenly, they lined up, turning their turrets toward the northwest, and began shooting their shells upon anything that moved. Caught rebel militia were lined up and executed on sight. If you didn't see the American flags, and the terrain was more temperate, then you could have thought you were in Yugoslavia during the Serbs' war on Bosnia. The clear blue skies of Las Vegas were no more. Just a reddish brown hue of smoke filled the air with its spewing of gray ash.

As the government tanks continued to unleash their destructive sweep, suddenly, a group of civilian rebels came from the rubble and began hurling Molotov cocktails.

The cocktails ignited several of the tanks along Sahara. As the government soldiers tried to escape from their inferno-engulfed tanks, they were quickly mowed down by the the rebels.

But then government Apache helicopters arrived at the scene and began launching rockets at these brave rebels. Several dozen rebels were blown away from the helicopters' rockets. But suddenly, two young rebels from a rooftop launched small guided rockets at the government helicopters, thus destroying them in mid-air.

But more government tanks and helicopters arrived, so the rebels retreated within the rubble. And the attritional tactic of guerilla warfare was now applied by these young rebels. Mind you, these rebels weren't soldiers, but the mixture a diverse group of Asian, black, Hispanic, and white young gang members. These gang bangers of Las Vegas had unified in the struggle against the government. These young rebels were now the *Resistance* of East Las Vegas.

But then the government tanks retreated back as a barrage of artillery began pounding East Las Vegas.

Meanwhile, the rebel forces positioned artillery gunners along Eastern Avenue in Las Vegas and began to counter with a volley of shells at the government's artillery positions in Henderson, a town just southeast of Las Vegas.

The battle for Las Vegas continued as the combined rebel forces with the *Resistance* stubbornly fought off every strike by the government forces with an equal counterstrike.

At 6:00 A.M. in southern Pennsylvania, from the southern horizon, several cruise missiles with their trailing tails were on their approach toward their targets, when suddenly they mysteriously disappeared.

At a government command post in Virginia, a startled Air Force soldier pulled off his headphones and shouted, "Sir, we have a problem. All of the eagles are off screen."

A general approached the young soldier and asked, "See if they were intercepted."

"Yes, sir." The soldier, with his headgear back on, punched away on his keyboard while looking at his monitor. He replied, "Sir, all of the eagles are lost. They... They just vanished, sir."

"Damn, they must've been intercepted!" the general shouted. He picked up the phone and then commanded into the receiver, "Armageddon is on! I repeat, Armageddon is on!"

Suddenly, a flashing series of outbursts came from southern Pennsylvania as government artillery gunneries continued discharging their shells into Pennsylvania skies. Their shells quickly descended, with them their destructive force.

The Eastern Alliance returned with their answer of artillery power.

Then, in the deep blue sky over southern Pennsylvania, hundreds of squadrons of government fighter and bomber jets approached. Suddenly, from a lead squadron startlingly blurted, "What the Sam hell is that?"

In full view before the squadrons in the northern and eastern horizons were several thousand F-16 and F-15 fighter jets, and below awaiting the government forces' approach was a mass arsenal of rebel forces composed of Apache helicopters, tanks, infantry, and artillery. The government forces in flight were in shock.

"Melonman to bird's nest. Melonman to bird's nest..." the lead squadron commander called.

"Bird's nest. Come in, Melonman," an officer responded in the northeastern government command center in a base in the mountains of West Virginia.

"Bird's nest. The rabbits have multiplied. I repeat, the rabbits have multiplied. I am transferring visual now. Acknowledge if you receive."

On a monitor before the officer, visual images of both the rebel ground and air forces came into view. "Acknowledged. Received. Stand by..."

The officer turned behind him and declared, "Commander, the rebel forces were underestimated by the AWACs. We just received this from point."

The general looked at the screen in total surprise, seeing the rows of tanks, helicopters, jet fighters, artillery, and missile launchers, "Holy shit! Where the hell did they all come from? Major, tell point not to proceed until we give further notice."

"Yes, sir," the officer replied.

The government general again viewed the monitor, still seeing thousands upon thousands of jets and helicopters in the southern skies of Pennsylvania, and then requested "Get me the president!"

An officer with an earphone on his head punched away on his communicator. Moments later, he responded, "Sir, no one is answering."

"What? What the fuck are you talking about?" the general returned, then grabbed the headphones and then redialed himself. The line was still dead. No answer.

"Shit! Damn communications! Tell point to continue to maintain their positions, but also notify ground to maintain their positions as well until I say otherwise. Armageddon is on hold."

The officer acknowledged, "Yes, sir."

The general looked back at the monitor again, and then he saw next to a rebel missile launcher, a sign that said "Gettysburg." The general shook his head in total awe of the situation.

At 11:00 A.M., in southern Nevada, the government forces continued their flattening of Las Vegas with a barrage of artillery and rocket fire, while in eastern Las Vegas, all along Charleston Avenue lay the remains of burning government tanks.

The scattered *Resistance* continued their "cat and mouse" attacks, frustrating the government army ground forces from permanently entering Las Vegas while a series of artillery and missile rockets continued to crush eastern Las Vegas in an attempt to subdue the *Resistance.*

Meanwhile, a Canadian mechanized division had entered into Utah from Colorado after seizing NORAD under a coordinated attack with the "rebel" Rangers and Airborne divisions. The Airborne and Rangers were now bearing down, setting up a defensive position in anticipation of any counterattack by government forces from the east to retake NORAD. The Canadians now continued their advance toward the southwest to Las Vegas.

The government forces were now beginning to encircle Las Vegas with a massive offensive toward North Las Vegas trying to split Nellis Air Force Base from North Las Vegas. The rebel forces continued to resist, trying to counter every attack from the government forces, but the continued pounding from the government's artillery began to take its toll, softening any response from the rebels.

But just as the government forces with their continual pounding and exploding arrived at the gates of Nellis, there was an awe of sudden silence. The government attacks had suddenly ceased. The rebel forces, perplexed by the sudden cease fire, were astonishment as the government forces began to withdraw.

From the east, the Canadian mechanized infantry with their mobile artillery units were thought to be no match for the government forces. But the Canadians, from a distance, lowered their turrets of the artillery gunners like tanks and unleashed their shells with precision, disseminating the rear division of government tanks. The Canadians' mechanized divisions slowly and methodically approached Las Vegas, while the government forces proceeded in a quick withdrawal, heading south into Arizona.

The rebel and *Resistance* forces celebrated as their Canadian allies entered into what was left of Las Vegas. People came out into the streets and began celebrating, cheering their Canadian neighbors.

As the Canadian armored personnel with rows of infantry entered The Strip, joined by the rebel forces, the people of Las Vegas began rushing and greeting the soldiers yelling, "God bless Canada! Long live the maple leaf! America is liberated! God bless America!"

Hundreds of soldiers, both American and Canadian, along with the people of Las Vegas begin to sing the song, "God Bless America."

CHAPTER 20

SELF-REALIZATION

Los Angeles... City of Angels...

During the battles of Las Vegas and Gettysburg, and the seizing of the White House, Kelly, John, and I remained in the War Operations facility in a bunker below the famous Chinese Theater.

We watched as Daniels and his associates were looking at maps and communicating on the phone to commanding officers who were at the front lines. Who would have thought that an actor would be coordinating military operations? But then who would've thought an actor would be President, yet Ronald Reagan became not only a Governor of California, but also the President of the United States. But come on, an actor/director/producer becoming a military leader? Life does have its surprises. But Daniels sure looked more like General George Patton than Marlon Brando when he made his monumental military decisions. I began teasing him, calling him Ike, and that really pissed him off, but then that wore off, so I had to come up with another name, though I never did.

I was certainly surprised how the American people finally rose up and took their destiny into their own hands. With ex-President Halliburton "exiled" back to Texas, a new, re-established government could now emerge in Washington. That is, a government of the people, by the people, and for the people could now persist as our forefathers had envisioned.

Since the fall of the White House, our rebel forces swiftly began to move south along the Eastern Seaboard. Within a week, our driving rebel forces of the East eventually swept all the way down south, taking control of Florida, Virginia, West Virginia, North and South Carolina, and Georgia. These Southern States quickly joined the new Union, allying themselves to the liberation movement and the reestablished government of the United States of America.

The United States of America was now united, with the exception of some remaining Southern and Midwestern States. The new front line bordered at Kansas and Missouri, which remained "Tory" to Halliburton.

Louisiana remained neutral, but would eventually make strides to come back to the Union.

Kansas, Oklahoma, Alabama, Mississippi, Kentucky, Nebraska, Iowa, Tennessee, Missouri, and Texas formed themselves into the United Christian States of America.

Looking back...

Reflecting....

It was just two weeks ago when a wonderful woman came into my life. Kelly, what a great woman... I felt so alive when I was with her. I guessed that love can do that to you. Even during these perilous times, we were constantly at each other's side, always supporting one another. Besides being my lover, Kelly became my best friend.

Kelly was so sweet, and for such a beautiful woman, she certainly had a warm heart.

I guessed that she was always on my mind, but not obsessively, more lovingly.

Like I said, we now were more partners in the arena of life than just simply passionate lovers. All right, I was just some dude who has fallen in love. Nothing special or unusual to most, except to those who are in love.

But, G-d almighty, I was falling in love with her, wasn't I?

Again looking back...

It wasn't long ago when I was just an average schmuck punching away on a computer, designing signs for a convention show, and today I was a celebrity. And all this was simply because... Because, I was on an alien starship...

So I wondered, whatever became of my alien friend, Yoshu'ah? He had said that so much will be changing, since their coming back to the

Earth plane, and so much did. I hoped that I will see him soon, because I have so much to ask.

While looking back on my life now, I realized that everything that had happened to me in the past was for a reason. Everyone's step in life, whether hard or easy, needs to be looked upon with acceptance, as opposed to with a struggle. With acceptance, all things are obtained with ease. In other words, "just ride the wave and don't swim against the current," and you'll get to your destiny with little effort. And that's why I was where I was supposed to be. Everything that has happened was created, so I would be where I am now. And I now knew and was quite aware of how blessed I am. I now looked forward to every event and every moment that lay before me.

"Thank you. Thank you, G-d... And thank you, the universe... Thank you..."

CHAPTER 21

JUST A DREAM

There was a hard knock at my door. I looked through the peephole. There were two middle-aged men dressed in gray suits. I asked from behind my front door, "Who are you?"

One of the men replied, "We are from the Internal Revenue Service. Are you Jerry Fletcher?!"

"What do you want with Jerry Fletcher?" I countered.

"We have to ask him a couple questions regarding his assets."

"Well... he isn't here!"

"Mr. Fletcher, don't be funny. We're authorized to levy your personal assets."

"Under what court order do you have the right to levy any of my property?!"

The two IRS agents chuckled and then one replied, "We don't need a court order. We're the IRS! Now open the door!"

"Go fuck yourselves!"

Suddenly, the agents kicked in my front door. I then dashed into my bedroom and grabbed my Browning 9mm automatic pistol.

The agents pulled their weapons out and begin discharging in my direction. In what seemed like slow motion, as if time had just slowed up, I fell to the ground as their missing bullets of death glanced over me, striking the wall behind. I pointed my pistol at the agents and unloaded four shots. My bullets pierced their skulls, exploding their bone fragments and flesh bits against the wall behind them.

Within moments, I heard from outside Metro Police officers, blasting out on a bullhorn, "Put down your weapon and come out with your hands on your head."

I slowly opened the door with my hands on my head, and, suddenly, Metro began firing their guns toward me. I quickly ducked back into my apartment.

While blood was rolling down my left shoulder, I grabbed my twelve-gauge and began returning fire toward the Metro Police.

Metro began blasting tear gas canisters through my window. The stinging fog quickly engulfed my apartment.

I crawled on the ground while maintaining my position. Four SWAT officers barged their way into my apartment, and I unloaded two shots from my twelve-gauge shotgun. Their heads were blown clean off from their necks.

Suddenly, my apartment was ablaze, so I began cutting a hole though the back wall of the apartment and then another hole was cut through the floor of the adjacent apartment. While sliding through, still holding my twelve-gauge and pistol, I discreetly opened the door of the apartment.

The apartment building was now a "Waco weenie roast." When all was clear, I slipped out while heading behind Metro forces as they continued to unload their weapons. My apartment building continued its blazing inferno.

A Metro officer yelled out, "Burn, baby, burn!"

The building collapsed.

"Jerry... Jerry... Are you okay?" Kelly whispered while stroking my forehead as I tossed and turned in my sleep. I then opened my eyes. "Jerry... Baby, you were having a nightmare." Kelly kissed my forehead.

I was startled, "Huh? What?"

"You were having a nightmare."

"Oh." I felt my sweaty forehead. Drops of sweat were running down the side of my head. "I felt like I ran a mile."

Kelly cuddled me, "Baby, I love you."

I smiled and then kissed her lips.

"Baby, you have to get ready. You have your big day at Las Vegas."

"Oh, yeah, the Las Vegas Memorial... Oh, God, I feel like shit."

"I'll heat up some coffee. You'll feel a lot better then."

"Thanks. I could use a fix of some caffeine," I replied while tapping my vein on the fold of my arm.

Moments later, while I was slowly sipping on some aromatic Turkish coffee, the doorbell suddenly rang but with a screeching sound like someone were running their fingernails down a chalkboard. Yeah, I know. The doorbell needs to be fixed. I'll get to it when I come back from Las Vegas.

I opened the door, and there were several men and women in suits, my security escort team.

One of the security men said, "I'm sorry, Senator, but your doorbell isn't..."

I interrupted, "Working. I know, but thanks."

A security woman approached me. "Senator, your car is right over here."

While Kelly and I were getting in a black limousine, photographers were flashing away, taking pictures like I was at the Academy Awards.

We then quickly spun off to Burbank Airport.

CHAPTER 22

TO NEW BEGINNINGS....

Over California....

While looking through the window of our cruising Learjet, Kelly was resting her head on my shoulder while I admired through the window the arid mountainous landscape down below.

I was on my way to Las Vegas to give a speech commemorating the emotional oration which I had given a year ago, when the Second American Revolution had erupted.

A lot has happened since then. Yeah, I wouldn't believe it myself, but I was now a U.S. Senator of California.

Halliburton still had control of Texas, while all the other remaining States eventually rejoined the Union.

We immediately initiated a tax reform bill that abolished the IRS and income tax, but created a flat value-added tax of 15% on all products sold and/or services rendered with the exception of food, rent below $800 per month and clothes that were $50 and below per item. Minimum wage was increased to $10 per hour and adjusted every two years with inflation. Individuals that had earned 1 million dollars in gross income in any given year would then be required to pay a 20% business tax in the subsequent following years (A maximum of ten years if gross yearly income falls below $50,000). Business tax was a flat 20% on gross income. Social Security was increased to 15% because it now included universal health care. Everyone now had health care. Health care was a right not a privilege. Also an incentive program that followed trickle economics that is from down up created a huge increase in income. This increase bought high purchasing revenue followed by a substantial increase in tax revenue which then helped cut by 50% the federal deficit that was created by Halliburton in his six years in office. Also the trade deficit was a thing of the past. In a nut shell, all and all, businesses and corporations flourished, while the individual also greatly benefited.

The cities were quickly rebuilt. Many of the States that were part of the Christian Coalition Government in Texas had chosen to rejoin the Union, because after a large exodus of people were trying to leave their States, Halliburton attempted to project a fence and wall to prevent any form of emigration. This was quickly foiled when our special militia units continually sabotaged any attempt to construct such a wall and/or fence.

Out of frustration, Halliburton had the audacity in attempting to detonate a nuclear warhead, but for some reason, all their nuclear devices seemed to malfunction. For some unexplained reason, the nuclear energy within the warheads collapsed within itself, leaving a heavy negative magnetic field.

Around the world, the violence had totally subsided. The world was at total peace, the first of its kind since King Solomon's rule of Israel. Could you believe that?

The perspective of the problem of drug use changed. Drugs were decriminalized. Drug addicts were treated as a mental disease. Drugs were distributed in an enclosed environment. Marijuana was taxed like alcohol. Growing any marijuana for distribution required a special permit and license, unless it was confirmed that it was for personal use and for medical reasons.

But the greatest change in America came by way of my Self-Love Self-Respect Education Act. This bill mandated that all schools, whether private or public, were required to have continual programs that taught and developed self-love and self-respect/self-esteem as part of the usual educational curriculum of general knowledge, reading, writing, and arithmetic. This education act alone almost overnight changed our civilization as we knew it. Even attitudes of adults were affected indirectly from their children. Talk about the kids teaching the adults. Who would have ever thought? Crime drastically dropped.

The economy was not only stable, but poverty was almost nonexistent.

Yes of course, we still had our crime. Like for example, when the new tax reform was initiated, some business owners tried to hide what was really sold or rendered, but with "due process" of the new court system, they were quickly prosecuted. The offenders were not imprisoned, but were sentenced with a mandatory community service, like cleaning the roads and trash or helping the poor financially, etc. Of course, those who didn't want to perform community service still had the option to perform community services in prison. It wasn't servitude, but all convicted criminals were required under their terms of their sentencing to pay retribution to their victims. So regarding the issue of tax fraud, the People of the United States would be considered victims on a whole, so then payment of retribution was applied to helping or performing services for the community.

Capital punishment could only be initiated if conclusive DNA evidence and visual evidence warranted it. By the way, child molestation was considered as heinous as first degree murder, and therefore, it could warrant capital punishment. But since the new Education Act, crime, like I said, was significantly down.

Oh, by the way, health insurance was nationalized. Oh yeah, I already mentioned that...

The Electoral College system was abolished, while campaign funding was strictly regulated and enforced, so that no plutocracy could emerge. Also, all television stations at their expense were required to give an equal amount of advertising time to all candidates running for public office. Campaign reform was also initiated. No monies were to be distributed to a prospective candidate for the benefit of any campaign for public office. People were really scared when this act was initiated. But then true candidates came forth, not confined to the interests of special interest groups.

The Bill of Rights was taken seriously and seriously followed.

Judges and prosecutors were not immune to malicious behavior. Free speech was extended to include the courtroom. Contempt of court only applied to court orders and a disruption of the courtroom proceedings, and not because you tell the judge that he or she is full of shit.

Contempt to a police officer was found unconstitutional.

So a lot has changed...

Now, money was slowly evolving into a non-issue while continual personal growth as a person as well as knowledge was becoming the major goal for the populace.

Movies and television still continued to entertain us in a free, unrestricted forum.

Television was now connected to the Internet. There were no restrictions on material except that all material must be graded for standard of violence and sex. The material was then given a rating which was locked in the visual computer file. This enabled a parent to choose in initiating parental control on the television. By the way, all televisions were required to have this parental control system feature. This made parents as well as the entertainment industry quite happy.

So after a year in office, change was amazingly welcomed.

But it was just a year ago that I was just a nine-to-fiver, and now today, I was a U.S. Senator. It was like opportunity and life had chased my ass down, and now here I was.

We were truly the product of what we feel and think. The universe has a way of giving back what we truly believe and think, so if you feel and think a certain way, then you will get exactly what you thought and felt, thus what you created. Remarkable isn't it?

DING! DING! DING!... The bell in the jet was ringing.

"Sorry, Senator, we're about to land. You'll have to buckle up," the flight attendant requested.

Las Vegas....

UNLV campus...

Thousands of people of every ethnicity and age group were crowded in and around an open area before a long temporary stage with a podium at its center.

People began chanting out loud, "Fletcher!!! Fletcher!!! Fletcher!!! Fletcher!!!"

A young man with a long ponytail approached the microphone and began to announce, "I would like to introduce to you, the man who initiated and helped lead us in the revolution for freedom, liberty, and justice in our great nation, the United States of America..."

The anticipating audience cheered.

The man at the podium then continued, "This man, during his first year in office as a United States Senator, has created and established the Flat Value Added Tax Act which abolished Internal Revenue Service and income tax."

Again the audience cheered.

The man at the podium again continued, "He also inspired and created a new platform for education by mandating a curriculum that includes the development of self-love, self-respect, and self-esteem, besides general knowledge and the basic fundamentals of reading, writing, and arithmetic. His new curriculum has drastically reduced crime and poverty. You are all aware of his many attributes for a better and more loving society.

"On this day, May fifteenth, exactly a year ago, Jerry Fletcher gave a speech about the truth, the DARK SIDE of organized religion, and the corporate intercourse with government. He elaborated about the inconsistencies and the lies of our prior government and system which did not follow the democratic system that was designed by our forefathers. His speech was the catalyst that woke up the American people. Thanks to him, we are no longer a nation of sheep."

"Fletcher!!! Fletcher!!! Fletcher!!!" The audience now chanted out. "Fletcher!!! Fletcher!!! Fletcher!" This chanting seemed to literally echo across the campus.

Under the continual chanting, the man then shouted back, "Here is a great man, a great humanitarian, and a great Senator. I bring you, Senator Jerry Fletcher!"

The audience screamed with cheers and then continued to chant again, "Fletcher!!! Fletcher!!! Fletcher!!!"

With Kelly and my daughter, Roxanne, at my side, I approached the podium, and then suddenly the audience was so quiet that you could drop a needle and everyone would hear it.

I began, "I'm... I'm simply blown away by all the..."

"You go, Jerry! You go!" Someone from the audience shouted out, and everyone laughed.

I cleared my throat and tried to begin, "I want to give a moment of silence for all those who died in the liberation. This includes those who perished in support of the prior government. G-d bless all those who perished. Please, a moment of silence."

Everyone maintained a moment of silence. It was so quiet that you could hear the gentle breeze ruffling the surrounding trees.

"Thank you." I momentarily paused and then replied, "This moment reminds me of a great passage from the *Tao Te Ching*. It is said that 'a great nation is like a great man: When he makes a mistake, he realizes it. Having realized it, he admits it. Having admitted it, he corrects it. He considers those that point out his faults as his most benevolent teacher. He thinks of his enemy as the shadow that he himself casts. If a nation is centered in the Tao, if it nourishes its own people and doesn't meddle in the affairs of others, it will be a light to all other nations in the world.'" And then there was a great applause.

After the applause subsided, I continued, "Therefore I say, 'let go of the law, and people become honest. Let go of economics, and people become prosperous. Let go of religion, and people become serene. Let go of all desire for the common good, and the good becomes common as grass.'"

Again there was applause and I continued, "I want to thank G-d and the universe for the opportunity that was given to us to pursue our liberty and freedom. Today, I'm not just proud to be an American, but I'm more proud of being a human being. LIGHT has truly shined upon Mother Earth. The angels of the universe, I thank you. I thank the angels of the LIGHT for my close encounter with the angelic extraterrestrials."

The audience was still totally focused upon my words as I continued, "When one great star soul told me 'Holy, Holy, Holy... Lord of Hosts...'

I did not understand then, but on this day I do. Thank G-d... The angels have risen!"

Suddenly, within the deep blue sky, a heavy white cloud began to swirl. People looked with astonishment at the sky as the cloud centered above suddenly opened up with a golden ray of illuminating light from within the center. An illuminating violet light began to emerge from within the golden light. Suddenly, forty aliens with white light emitting from their backs were descending upon the open area. People continued to just stare at the amazing biblical-like show. Finally, five of the aliens descended upon the stage. One of them was Yoshu'ah.

The five aliens, including Yoshu'ah, approached me.

"Kadosh, Kadosh, Kadosh... Adonai Tsva'ot." Yoshu'ah declared while holding up both his palms, spreading his fingers to form a "V."

I smiled.

He then announced, "The Earth souls are now ready for new wisdom, new knowledge to help them to continue on their path toward the LIGHT." Yoshu'ah then approached me and asked, "Are you ready to return? Your mission is now complete."

"My mission?" I replied, bewildered.

"Sorry, love, but he was talking to me," Kelly answered.

"What? You're an alien?" I asked, surprised.

"Yeah... Actually I'm Pleaidian."

"So all this time, I was just part of your mission? Our relationship was simply part of your plan?" I lashed out.

"At first, but then I fell." A tear rolled down her cheek as she continued. "But then, I fell in love with you. I'm sorry, but..."

I looked down, confused by what was now explained to me, and then she held my hand. "Jerry, I love you so much. I'm so sorry, but at the time, it was for the best. Only John knew who I was."

"And your grandmother dying, was that all a lie too?" I snapped back.

Kelly looked into my eyes. "She was really my mother." And with tearful eyes, she looked down, "She was... She was my mother."

I then compassionately took hold of her hand.

Kelly, still tearful, looked into my eyes then kissed my cheek and emotionally replied, "Jerry, I love you. I want to be with you forever. I don't want to leave you. I love you."

Yoshu'ah interjected, "Jerry, you're more than welcome to join us."

I looked into Kelly's eyes, and my eyes began to tear. "I could not live a moment with the thought that I just walked away from my precious soul mate. Kelly, I love you."

"Does that mean yes?" Kelly asked with a doe-eyed look.

I kissed her lips then looked into her eyes while replying, "Yes."

Kelly kissed me.

I discreetly whispered in her ear, "So for a year, I've been fucking an alien. I hope I didn't get any alien V.D."

Kelly poked me in the rib cage with her elbow. "I don't know how I can love so much, because sometimes you can be such an asshole."

We gently kissed each other's lips and I said, "I love you."

Kelly, while holding me, passionately kissed me.

An illuminating violet light began whirling around us as we continued in our embrace. Suddenly, Kelly and I were now airborne, ascending in the ray of illuminating violet light to the awaiting starship above.

Isaiah 2.2
In the days to come,
The Mount of the Lord's House
Shall stand firm above the mountains
And tower above the hills;
And all nations
shall gaze on it with joy.

And the many peoples shall go and say:
"Come, Let us go up to the Mount of the Lord,
To the House of the G-d of Jacob;
That He may instruct us in his ways,
For instruction shall come forth Zion,
The word of the Lord from Jerusalem.
Thus nations He will judge among nations
And arbitrate for the many peoples,
And they shall beat their swords into plowshares
And their spears into pruning hooks:
Nation shall not take up
Sword against nation;
They shall never again know war.

THE END

I THINK...

NOT REALLY...

NOTHING EVER REALLY ENDS...

EVERYTHING JUST CONTINUES....

BUT WHAT IF?...

WELL, ANYWAY, G-D BLESS YOU...................

ABOUT THE AUTHOR

Having lived several lives in one, Andrew Feder during the eighties lived in Israel on a Moshav for six years as a grape farmer, and after returning to the United States, for the next ten years, he was a contractor and owner of a construction company. In the late nineties, he drove a cab and a limo during hiatus while working as an assistant director in the film industry. At the end of the nineties, he moved to Las Vegas from Los Angeles, where for one year, he was (and hates to admit it) a "damn" telemarketer selling long distance, and for the past five years he's been a graphic artist.

From his college years, he wrote several editorials and short stories. Much later, during the so-called midlife crisis, he evolved in his development to include writing both novels and poems along with subsequent screenplays.

Printed in the United States
69083LVS00003B/142-144